FORGIVEN

Book Two
Worth Fighting For Series

By Kelly Hagen

Published by TreasureLine Publishing
www.TreasureLinePublishing.weebly.com

Cover Design by Michele Barrow-Belisle

CHAPTER ONE

Taking over a family line was never an easy task to accomplish, even for a high ranking demon. There was a system, a protocol to how things worked. People were tested. Tried to see if they could be used for the dark purpose intended for them. Such had been done with the Burnsten family. Careful steps had been taken to make sure each of them held a deep darkness ruled by pride and selfishness, hate, and manipulation. For it was those very qualities, bred over time, that would lead to the ultimate self-righteousness that was needed to drive the coming rebellion that was almost a century in the making.

Melti thought back to the day Latar had visited him and told of the Head Master's plan, a plan that would lead to the takeover of all Green Hill. One that would slowly but surely progress until all of Kentucky and its surrounding towns, cities, and states had made their pledge to the Master's side. This would take time, but what were a few hundred years when all eternity was hanging in the balance?

All had progressed nicely until nineteen years ago. The enemy, that glory-filled heavenly being, had stepped in and changed the course of everything, destroying Latar in the process.

But now, now the future of the Burnsten line once again

stood a chance of thriving, thanks to the black-haired, green-eyed, teenage daughter of none other than Katelyn Burnsten herself. It made no difference that she went by Holcomb these days, the same Burnsten blood ran through her veins, and through the veins of her sixteen-year-old daughter.

Unbeknownst to Celeste Holcomb, her time of testing had finally come. She had reached the age where one could easily be tempted – ever so cautiously swayed from the path she was on to one that would drag her deep into a different calling – one of vengeance, rebellion, and greed.

Melti shook the looming thoughts of failure from his mind, and instead let his thoughts wander back in time, almost a year to date, to be exact. The seeking spirits he'd sent out daily had brought back news of two boys, brothers, one getting ready to head into foster care. It seemed their parents weren't all that concerned with caring for the needs of their children since a specific substance had been introduced in their lives a couple of years prior. Drugs, how they could work wonders.

Mack had been doing the best he could to keep his younger brother Daren out of trouble, but it wasn't going so well. At least not in their hometown.

Melti liked what he had seen hidden deep down in the younger boy. His parents' betrayal had affected him far more than it had his older brother. Daren's young heart, once so full of love and trust was now hard and full of bitterness. Just the way Melti liked them.

Melti was sure Daren would be of great assistance in veering Celeste off track. What young girl could resist good looks followed up with some deceiving charm? Very few.

Getting these two boys to the little country town of Green Hill wasn't all that hard to do since they were just a county over. Mack and his concern for his brother was a big help in making it all come together. He took responsibility for

Daren so he wouldn't be placed in a home. Only Heaven knew what would've happened to him if that were the case.

Melti had whispered an idea into Mack's thoughts and next thing you know a semi-run down, two-story house in Green Hill, was now where the boys laid their heads and called home.

Melti went to great lengths not only to find a job opening that would keep Mack very busy and out of his way, but also to make sure Daren, after the students return from break one week later, was in some of Celeste's classes, leaving their odds of running into each other at pretty much one-hundred percent. Though by mere happenchance Daren had met Celeste the day he and Mack had moved in. Melti couldn't have been more pleased if he'd thought of that "by chance meeting" himself.

The Holcomb's had been visiting Katelyn's dad, who lived in her departed Aunt Cara's old house, which just happened to be the neighboring place to Mack and Daren's new dwelling. Daren had taken a walk through the woods and came out the other side, only to be stopped in his tracks by the young girl a few feet away. She looked to be trying to keep herself occupied while those he assumed to be her parents said their goodbyes to an older man standing on the porch of the house several feet behind her. He stood still too long and was seen by the girl, who slowly made her way in his direction.

And so it began.

The couple seeds of doubt and a cute, persuasive boy were a few means by which the attempt to win the young girl over would begin. Though small on their own, each played a meaningful part in the plan to put the evil claim back where it belonged. It was for that very reason Melti took a long moment and embraced the grotesque, morbid sense of satisfaction that snaked its way through his hideous frame.

Waiting had never been a strong suit for any demon, but especially not for Melti. Now, though, he was able to rest a little easier, as the pawns on his imaginary chessboard were moving into place.

Relationships had been started. Deceit would soon be wedged, ever so slightly, into the frail beating of the human hearts that were his targets. Unforeseen betrayal would rear its ugly head. Feelings would be hurt, and faith would be questioned. Melti was sure of it. With what he'd planned for Celeste's future, how could they not be? Everything just had to stay the course.

The boy would soon find the book. The girl had found the boy. And Hell had its mark. What more could a wretched being ask for?

Melti grinned, the points of his jagged teeth slightly exposed under the rim of the charcoal leather that was his skin. He called for Deception. It was time for the next piece of the puzzle to be put into place. Deception bowed as he came to a stop in front of Melti's desk. "You called for me, master."

"Yes. It's time, Deception. It is your turn to take the torch." Thin, gray lids came almost to a close over Melti's yellow eyes...his voice low, full of authority. "Do. Not. Fail. Me. Now go!"

"Yes, master," Deception answered.

Melti scratched a deep groove across the desk in front of him with the pointed tip of his nail and watched in vague amusement as the spirit quickly fled from his presence, only to have the same amusement, seconds later, replaced with sudden thoughts of failure again. That very thought sent vibrations up and down the woven chords in his thick neck, causing the release of a deep snarl. Muscles tensed, stretching out the dark skin that covered them. It was his neck on the chopping block this time around. Failure of his subordinates would not be accepted. It couldn't be. His very existence was on the line.

Nothing worth having ever came easy, Melti was well aware of that nagging little fact, and if Katelyn was no longer in the crosshairs, then her precious daughter, Celeste was the next best thing.

That one piece, one tiny little piece, was all that remained.

It was strange, that so much rode on such a frail mortal. But this family. This line. This *Celeste* needed to be in place before future events could unfold.

Deception crept near the ground like a slow, methodical snake inching its way through a protective covering of tall, swaying grass. He weaved this way and that through the objects that surrounded him. Hidden well by the cover of darkness, for it consumed the wispy edges of his smoke-colored body. Beady eyes darted frantically to and fro seeking out their destination.

A wide grin split open his dry, cracked lips, causing a moist red line to appear. He didn't care. His mission was close by. He could feel it. Deception came to a stop near a two-story brick home. He knew he'd reached the right location from the doubt that saturated the air.

He slowly edged his way around the corner, and there, a mere ten-feet away, stood his target clothed in a black sweater and faded blue jeans, so oblivious of what was to come. Though Deception was honored to be a part of such a critical mission, he was careful not to think of himself more highly than he ought. He knew just how quickly things could go wrong. He'd seen it happen before and he wanted nothing to do with it again. He'd been a part of the original plan that had involved Katelyn, and that plan hadn't ended well. At least not for his side. They'd lost yet another soul to Heaven that night, along with their leader, Latar. Losing this target, he knew, was out of the question.

That hard lesson with its high price to pay was forever etched into Deception's memory. From that moment on he never assumed everything would work out just because it all appeared to be going as planned. Appearance, it could be a tricky thing.

CHAPTER TWO

Celeste tried to focus on the words written in red that lined the thin page before her. It was not easy. The digitized numbers across the room, the very thing that kept interrupting her focus, had changed yet again. The time had come, leaving only mere minutes to make a final decision. *What am I thinking? I can't honestly be getting ready to sneak out? Can I?*

A few flips of the crinkly pages led to a small photo that had captured the handsome face, which was the cause of her fluttering heart and indecisiveness. The printed colors on the glossy paper had in no way done justice to the bright green color of his eyes. *Way more appealing than the deep green hues of my own that's for sure.*

Tiny hairs covered a strong jawline and led up the side of his face to thick, brown hair that came just past his ears, and short bangs that were slightly swooshed to the side. How could she ever say no to that?

The very essence of "bad boy" rang loud and clear through his stare. Wild, yet controlled. Dark, yet bright. Tough, yet gentle. Those perfectly parted lips knew what to say and when to say it. So persistent and persuasive. She closed the Bible that was on her lap and laid it on her nightstand. Then she tucked a body pillow under the soft orange comforter that covered the full-size bed. With one last deep breath the choice had been made, and with it, the window opened.

"I guess I am."

Daren had won again.

Daren grabbed Celeste's hand and lead her through the front doorway of his house. He tightened his grip around her fingers – a small gesture to drive out any last minute fears that could be swarming their way through her head. He hoped it worked. Unfortunately, her forced smile said otherwise. *This may be harder than I planned.*

"Come on Cee, it will be alright. I have something I want to show you. I found it behind the old farmhouse next door." He twirled his finger around his ear, "you know, the one your mom's crazy aunt use to live in." By the scowl on Celeste's face, he knew he had made his point, but she did not care for it. *Great, strike two.*

"Yeah, I know the house," Celeste answered. "What were you doing there?"

Daren shrugged his shoulders and let his sideways grin work its magic. He knew just how to distract the naive girl in front of him. Her type was always so easy to read. The longing for acceptance in her facial features actually saddened him for a mere second. Though she tried her best to hide it, she needed some practice. Her weakness, her vulnerability would be his greatest weapon, and he had every intention of using it against her.

"They say that place is haunted. You know that, right?"

"Oh, please." Daren chuckled. "A little weird stuff isn't going to scare me away. "

"Well, maybe it should," she said, voice quaking. "Never mind. What was it you wanted to show me?"

"It's in my room, come on." Daren turned and headed for the steps, taking them two at a time. He stopped when he hadn't heard the protests of the squeaking stairs a second time from her following behind him. He turned back. Celeste had remained motionless, watching him. His brows rose in question.

"I think I'll stay down here if that's alright with you," Celeste said.

"Suit yourself. Not sure when Mack will be coming in though." Swaying her feelings had never been a hard thing to do. Her resolve would diminish. Sometimes he had to push a little harder, but his scare tactic would work in the end. It always did.

"Fine," she huffed. Her pace on the stairs was much slower than Daren's. He knew her well. Knew she was, at that very moment, questioning herself. They had been down this road several times already. Yet, her desire to please him had won every time.

Daren waited as Celeste hesitantly stepped through the open doorway and over to the side so he could follow. The door clicked behind them. Her body stiffened. He ignored it.

"Have a seat." He patted the unmade bed before kneeling down to grab something from underneath it. Particles filled the air between them as he wiped off the thin layer of dust. "Ready?" He asked.

"Yes." The apprehension in her eyes betrayed her response.

He handed the book out for Celeste to take. Her fingers traced the raised leather design on the cover. "What is this?" she asked.

"I'm not sure. I was hoping we could look it up together." Daren didn't bother to hide his excitement. "I think it might have something to do with some sort of code or something?"

Daren took the book from Celeste's trembling hands. He flipped it open to the first page and ran his finger under the single word boldly written in the center of the crinkled yellow paper.

Celeste gasped, "Satan," she whispered.

Daren cocked his head to the side. "How did you know what it said?"

Celeste shrugged as if it were nothing. "I've been learning several old languages. This was one of my most recent words." She focused her gaze on the book once again. "My mom and I wanted to be able to read the Bible in its original language, and so we just decided to learn some other ones while we were at it."

Not again.

Why she had to keep ruining perfectly sane moments with such nonsense he'd never understand. If it wasn't for the hope of finding out more about the book, this Bible reference probably would have been her last.

"I see. So, do you think you would be able to read the rest of it, then? At least some of it anyway?" His interest surprised her.

"I do not know. Not sure I want to."

"Why not?"

"Daren, really? You know I don't like this kind of stuff. I mean, I won't even watch most of the movies you want to about this kind of thing, why would I want to read about it?"

Her holier-than-thou attitude was not her intention. Deep down he knew that, yet it still frustrated him. Daren knew he had been pressuring her pretty hard as of late, so he let it go. He had gotten her in his room alone with him. A major breakthrough.

"It would be a way we could hang out more," he said.

"How so?"

"Just tell your parents we have to research information on an old book or something. You are a creative girl. I'm sure you can come up with a good excuse."

"You know they would want it done at my house."

"Well, just think about it."

"Alright, I'll think about it."

Who's she trying to kid. She'll do it. We both know it.

"Awesome." Daren leaned in and kissed the top of her head, then replaced his newly found interest back in its former spot.

"Are we done now? I would like to go back downstairs, if that's okay?" she whispered.

"Really? We have time alone, and you want to go downstairs?" He took her hand and gently pulled her up from the edge of the bed. A lone curl had fallen in front of her face, and he tucked it behind her ear. Her erratic breathing matched his own. Pushing her over the edge would be easy. Yet, he didn't. He needed her trust. He'd bide his time, for now.

Instead, he laced his fingers with hers, "Yeah, it's okay. Come on."

A low rumble filled the air outside as they descended the stairs. Mack was home. Great. So much for sneaking Celeste back to her house without anyone the wiser.

"Whoa, there little bro, where do you think you're going?"

"I was going to walk Celeste home."

Daren stood a moment under his brother's gaze before attempting to move around him. A tight grip on his shoulder caused him to flinch and stop mid-step. He did not turn around, just stood to wait. Waiting for what, he wasn't sure. With Mack, it could be good or bad, depending on how his night had gone.

"What kind of big brother would I be if I let you walk

11

her home in the dark?" Mack chuckled. Daren tried to hide his sigh of relief but didn't think he pulled it off. At that moment he really did not care. Getting Celeste home was his only priority.

CHAPTER THREE

Celeste woke to the warm kiss of sunlight on her face. It was Saturday, and that meant one thing. A big breakfast would be spread out on the light brown table, waiting to be devoured by the three hungry mouths that sat around it. She inhaled deeply, the aroma of crispy bacon caused her relaxed body to stir within the blankets that cocooned her small frame.

She rubbed the sleep from her eyes and dared a glance at the clock. Nine thirty. Sleeping in was great.

"Smells good, Mom!" Celeste said as she entered the kitchen.

Katelyn smiled, "Good morning, Celeste."

She laughed when her mother asked if she was hungry. Two spoonfuls of eggs and several slices of bacon topped with a sweet, warm biscuit filled her plate.

"What gave it away?" Celeste laughed, at the raised eyebrow and grin that was on her mother's face.

"Well, I suppose we should pray then, so you can eat."

Celeste noticed her dad's absence, which was out of the ordinary. Saturday breakfasts were a Holcomb tradition. "Where's Dad?"

"Oh, Your grandpa moved the last of his boxes out of Aunt Cara's place last night. Who would have guessed after living there all these years that he'd choose to move out?

Anyway, so Dad woke a bit early this morning so he could get a head start on the few repairs that it needs before we can get that old place on the market and out of our hands. I'll be joining him in a little while. Would you like to come to help us?" Katelyn's hopeful tone and look didn't escape Celeste, but this was just the opportunity she had been waiting for, and spending time with her parents at that creepy house wasn't something she wanted on her agenda today, or any day for that matter.

"I'm sorry, Mom. I have a ton of homework. Would you mind if I stayed home?"

"Sure, honey. That's okay."

Disaster averted. Door opened. Celeste couldn't wait to call Daren. Hopefully, he would be able to meet up today.

"You can pick up your room if you need a break from your school work."

Celeste looked towards her mom. Sadness gripped at her heart for a long moment. It was becoming so easy to lie to them.

Like sand falling through loosely held fingers, the closeness, the openness they'd shared was slowly slipping away. At times, she even questioned Daren's warnings about so-called loving parents. Her mom and dad had never given her a reason to doubt their love or the love the Lord had for her.

"Celeste, you okay?"

"Oh, yeah, just thinking." At least that wasn't a lie. She'd been doing that a lot since meeting Daren. Somehow her feelings, her convictions were gradually becoming numb to her. She prayed less and hardly read the Bible anymore. Daren didn't believe in God – said if there were a "god" he'd be a sorry excuse of one with the way the world was today. That was nothing she hadn't heard before. Deep down Celeste knew otherwise, but was shot down anytime she tried to state differently. Keeping her faltering beliefs to herself had become the norm in this new life of hers.

"Celeste, did you hear a thing I said?" Her mother's concerned voice broke her silent train of thought. "No, Mom, sorry. What did you say?"

"I said your dad and I might not be back until late. There are a few things in the freezer you can heat up if you get hungry. Are you sure you're okay? I can stay here with you if you like."

"No, Mom, you don't need to stay here. I'm fine, really. If I get hungry, I'll find something to eat. Don't worry." She smiled like her life depended on it.

"Well, all right then. Will you please get these dishes put away before starting on your homework?" "Sure, Mom."

Celeste stood in the doorway and waved, watching as Katelyn backed out of the drive. The door remained open until the small two-door vehicle was no longer in sight.

Celeste set her breakfast dishes in the sink, and then ran up the stairs to grab her phone. Her finger slightly shook as she dialed Daren's number. The endless ringing made her insides crawl. Why wasn't he answering?

After several rings, she hung up and tried again. Nothing. It appeared her plans for the day had changed. Cleaning and homework, it was.

It was well after three when she stuffed her last book into the confines of her favorite, tattered backpack. Still no word from Daren. Strange. Against her better judgment, she redialed his number. Again...nothing. Her thoughts began to wander, taking her to places she didn't want to go. Jarred back to reality by the ringing of the house phone, she shook off the thoughts and picked up the noisy black device. "Hello?"

"Hey, sweetie," her mom's voice was full of cheer, as it always was. How can someone be so happy all the time? She couldn't for the life of her figure it out.

"Hey, Mom. How're things going?"

"Pretty good. Almost done for today. Pretty soon it will be ready to put on the market."

"That's great."

"We were going to pick up dinner on the way home. I was calling to see what sounds good to you?"

"Oh, I don't know. Whatever you guys want will be fine."

"You sure?"

"Yep." Celeste tried to cover her disappointment with her own cheery voice.

"Celeste?"

Curse her mom's intuition. "Really, Mom. Whatever you guys want is good with me. I just finished my school work, so I'm a little brain dead right now."

"Okay. We'll talk when we get home."

"About what?"

"About whatever is bothering you. Dad's calling for me. We'll see you shortly. Okay?"

"Okay, bye, Mom."

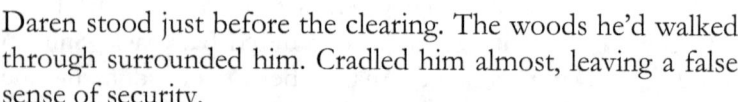

Daren stood just before the clearing. The woods he'd walked through surrounded him. Cradled him almost, leaving a false sense of security.

He stared at the white wooden house with two vehicles parked in its circular drive. A short, dark-haired woman trotted up the front porch steps, her ponytail swaying back and forth. Her eyes, a stunning blue, were on him before he knew it. He'd been caught, so there was no use hiding now, but he did anyway. Thoughts and emotions of all kinds flooded over him. Thoughts and emotions that he wasn't sure were his own, or where they'd even come from.

Daren had no idea how much time had passed before he peeked out from behind the tree, but when he did, the woman along with both cars was gone. He looked down at his phone, shocked. Not only had he missed calls from Celeste, but four hours had passed. Rough fingers slid down his face. "No way."

He made his way to the bench in his front yard sat down, and waited for Celeste to answer his call.

CHAPTER FOUR

Celeste knew Daren wouldn't even come close to passing her parents "study buddy" approval. Though Stacey, a close friend of hers definitely would – she had several times in the past. So unbeknownst to Katelyn and Trevor, Daren had become Stacey.

The fact that their masquerade had been going strong for a month or so now left Celeste a little on edge. Sooner or later this whole thing was bound to blow up in her face. And she wasn't looking forward to it. But as the old saying goes 'Nothing lasts forever.'

Celeste was seated next to Daren, reading over the book he'd found near her old family house. She hardly ever went around that place if she could help it. Even visiting with her grandpa had been preferred on less creepy ground. Not that she'd seen him all that often. His lifestyle, along with his job, had always kept him pretty busy. Maybe that was for the best?

Her mom talked to Grandpa at least once a week. Their conversations, the ones she had just happened to hear anyway, sounded tense and forced more than anything else. It had always been that way, ever since Celeste could remember.

Now that her Grandpa had moved south, seeking the warmer temperatures it held, she hopefully would never have to enter those four walls again. That was something in her turned upside-down world that she could definitely deal with.

Daren's mocking and constant jabs at her already dwindling faith were a little bit harder to handle. They were leaving her with questions she couldn't answer. Questions she had never considered before.

Everything she had been able to decipher so far in that dreadful book was the complete opposite of what she had been taught to believe. It was like the Bible she had grown up being so sure of had left out a large part of what really happened. As though it were a bit one-sided. That left a bitter taste in Celeste's mouth, along with a widening hole in her heart.

Had Lucifer's banishment from heaven really been necessary? He just wanted to please his Creator, show him how much he had learned. Prove that he could be a just and fair ruler. Right? At least that is the way the old brown book made things sound. Was it so bad for him to want and declare worship for himself as well? He was after all the most beautiful, talented, archangel. He had that right too...didn't he?

Am I really going there?

Celeste shook her head trying to make sense of her reasoning but failed miserably. Somewhere in this journey, bits of doubt had ever so slightly worked their way from a minute hole to an overly large crack, splitting the very foundation of everything she had ever known almost entirely in two, and leaving her once firm beliefs laced with immense skepticism.

Was it possible everything taught to her was a lie? Surely not. But how could a loving God consider the banishment of one of His best creations without giving a full account? There wasn't a full account given, was there? The fact that she could not remember had tiny beads of sweat trickling down her back, or maybe it was the afternoon sun – the late spring weather had increased the digits on the thermometer over the last couple days. *Yeah, that's what it is...not these crazy thoughts swirling around in my head.*

Celeste ran her palms up and down her pant legs, trying to focus on anything but the dance party going on in her stomach. She had to get away from Daren, away from that book. "I think I'm done for today, Daren. I need to get back home before my mom calls Stacey's to ask where I'm at."

She watched as Daren finished copying down a sentence then closed the book. "Yeah, my little angel is becoming quite the devil...isn't she?" He grinned as he ran his fingers through her hair. He gently cupped her neck and pulled her towards him. This wasn't the first time she had given in to his lips meeting hers.

◆ ◆ ◆ ◆ ◆

Silver-tipped wings slightly rustled back and forth, sending invisible, yet very present gleaming lines along the walls of Daren's dimly lit room. A scowl distorted the usually calm features of Jasie, Celeste's Guardian Angel's face. Brows once separated by a smooth skin were now separated by slight ridges between them. Eyes the deepest of brown glowed faintly with righteous disapproval.

Jasie whispered words of wisdom to Celeste, all the while ignoring the taunts and jeers from the enemies surrounding the youth across the room from him. He prayed to the Creator that they would reach his charge's ears.

Though, there had always been an irritating presence around Celeste. One they knew would be there, for it just came with the territory...life. It seemed to be growing darker. His covering was being pushed back inch by inch every day. More than the typical teenage "rebellion," this tension was strategic, there was no doubt. Something more menacing was going on behind all the recent events and choices his charge made. Too much was happening too fast.

He fought the stirred desire within him. Desire for the authority to put a stop to what was happening before him. Who knew if this would be it. The time Celeste did not have enough strength to fight her feelings. The time she did not tell the boy no. Why was it so hard for humans to see the enemy meddling in their lives? Were they honestly not able to understand what was at stake, or did they just not care?

How could they not?

Jasie let out a sigh of relief when Celeste's hand rose to Daren's chest and applied a small amount of pressure. The connection had been broken. A muffled growl filled the air. The boy was not happy. "I know, I'm sorry Daren. I just can't do this right now. Not yet." Those were not the words Jasie hoped to hear, but for tonight they would have to do.

"I really need to go, Daren. I'll text you when I get home, okay?"

Frustrated, was he, to say the least, but he responded well. No doubt for the sake of keeping Celeste in his firm grip. The amount of control Daren had over her decisions was unnerving.

"Hey, yeah, sure. Text me when you get home."

Celeste kissed Daren on the cheek. "Thank you for being so understanding." she said, then turned and walked away, her Guardian a few steps behind.

Jasie met Kanone on the front steps of the Holcomb's home a short while later. They both watched as Celeste took a deep breath and exchanged her very confused true self to one of a happy, carefree teenager. Unfortunately, she wore that mask well.

"I'm glad she is back on the guarded ground." Jasie let out a deep breath. He had not meant for his statement to sound so full of alarm, though it should, and it did.

"How did things go tonight?" Kanone asked.

Jasie wished he had a better answer to give his fellow Guardian, but that wasn't the case. "Not good," he responded and then went on to tell Kanone everything that had happened.

"Just as I feared," Kanone stated. "Seems like there is more at work in Celeste's life than just the meddling intrusion of Doubt and Deception. Melti and Ackmen may very well be behind all of this. If so, there will be a war. A war we cannot fight."

Jasie nodded, "I believe you are right, Kanone."

"I think it is time to request the Warriors."

CHAPTER FIVE

Necklim's eyes glowed gold as he made his way to the Throne room. For him to be summoned could only mean one thing – Melti was seeking the Burnsten family line – again.

He pushed open the sizeable golden door with ease and made his way across the room to the Commander's Throne. He bowed before the Creator; long, blonde strands of hair fell at either side of his face. Then he stood, shoulders squared, and waited for the Commander to speak.

"The time has come, Necklim. Melti has set in motion his plan for Celeste. Kanone has also sent word of a heaviness in the Holcomb household. Jasie, as you may know, was sent to guard Celeste, but his space around her has been decreasing more and more."

Necklim entertained the thought of bursting through the doors, descending on the earth, searching out his enemy's whereabouts and putting an end to Melti's evil existence once and for all, but instead asked the Commander what the assignment was. He'd hoped it was the scenario that had played out in his mind but doubted that was the case. At least not yet.

"I'll be sending in the Warriors. You, of course, will lead them," his Commander spoke, "but I want you to check it out first. There may be a need for more Warriors this time."

"Of course, Commander. I'm on my way." Necklim bowed again and turned to go, but stopped at his Commander's words.

"Necklim, be watchful."

"I will, my Lord. Watchful and ever ready."

Seconds later, Necklim gently landed on the Holcomb's front lawn. The blades of grass that once stood straight and tall now lay flat underneath the enormous weight of the heavenly being standing on top of them. He glanced over the front of the house, his gaze stopping on the knelt silhouette behind the curtain of the front bay window. "Help is on the way, Katelyn," he whispered.

Necklim appeared next to Kanone, who was standing over Katelyn. "What's been going on here?" he questioned.

Kanone folded his wings and turned to face Necklim, "There's a heaviness like we've never felt before. Celeste is becoming increasingly disconnected towards Katelyn and Trevor, which has led to an increase in their prayers."

"A darkness," Kanone continued, "is slowly surrounding Celeste. Jasie doesn't have as much of an area around her as he once had. It seems to be shrinking every day."

"That's not good."

"No, it is not."

Necklim looked around the room, sensing something was off, "We'll need not only their prayers but the prayers of their friends, families, and church. I sense an alarming presence here. Melti has had years to prepare for this moment. But so have we."

Necklim turned to Kanone. "Keep watch. I'll return soon with other Warriors."

Kanone nodded his head and returned to his protective stance over Katelyn.

A breeze whipped around Celeste. It stirred the new leaves on the nearby trees from their stillness. Then brushed against her face, sending goosebumps to raise and cover her arms.

It brought with it the promise of an evening rain shower. One she hoped would arrive soon. Rain – its rhythmic plops and dings as it fell against the different objects, the smell of the damp soil it left in its wake – had always been a form of comfort to her. Somewhat like a security blanket, strange as that may be. It worked in calming the overly active nerves that twisted and turned throughout the young teenage body. It was her hope it would bring that same calming effect tonight.

The sidewalk leading up to Daren's front door seemed more like a runway than a walkway. Lights evenly spaced rang along both sides of the pebbled concrete like a beacon leading one to safety. Safe...would that really be the way to describe the person inside? Of that, she wasn't sure.

Celeste had thought long and hard about what they'd do on their first night alone. Reading that dreadful book was not a part of the plan. Persuading him to focus on something else was.

Celeste raised her hand, hesitating only a moment before knocking.

"Hey, sorry, I was in the kitchen trying to find something for us to munch on. Mack hasn't been to the store this week, so there's not much in there."

"That's okay. I'm not hungry anyway." Eating at a time like this was not a good idea. Food on a nervous stomach never ended well.

Daren shrugged. "Okay, then. Let's head upstairs."

"Sure." She followed the boy that held her heart in the

palm of his hand up the steps, with a newly found sense of determination. Would it really be this easy?

"Hop on the bed, I'll get the book," he said as he bent over to grab the leather bound piece of history.

"Daren, I was hoping maybe we could do something else tonight?"

"Oh, yeah. Like what?" he asked, looking up at her. She knew he was trying to read her expression. Figure out just what she had in mind. For once it wasn't his lips that had overtaken hers, but hers that had overtaken his.

There was a soft plop on the bed beside her before a warm hand met her cheek. He was eager. Ready. There was no turning back now. If Celeste had really wanted this to happen or not was no longer a question. It was going to happen.

She pushed the book off the bed and pulled him towards her, only to be met with him pulling away. *Great, what did I do wrong?* "Daren?"

"Just scooting the book back under the bed. I don't want anything to happen to it."

An invisible blow struck her. Was Daren serious? He didn't just say that, did he? No, he couldn't have. Surely he knew how important this was. A gift, one not really wanting to be given, was being offered, yet this boy who'd taken over every waking thought in her young mind was still worried about that precious book? Celeste wasn't sure how these things went, but she was pretty confident it wasn't like this.

"Wait, what was that?" Daren disappeared only to reappear seconds later with a folded paper in his hand. He sat next to her, opened it, and started to read.

Celeste stared at him in disbelief. Her heart ached in ways she'd never known possible. Painful, raw, emotions inside broke free and slid down her face. She let them fall. Who cared if he thought it showed weakness. Maybe she was weak. "Really, Daren?"

Celeste rose and stomped across the floor fully intending to leave Daren behind in his own little world, but was stopped just shy of the door by the tone she'd heard in his voice. It was one she hadn't heard before. "I think you'll want to read this."

Jasie wasn't sure if he should thank the meddling mist that was Deception for that slight breeze that just so happened to knock the folded paper from the book and onto the floor. It may have stopped one lousy experience from taking place, though his concern was how bad the one that would become of it would end up being. From Celeste's crinkled nose and pulled low brows, it wasn't going to be good. Betrayal laced the only word that Celeste had whispered, "Mom?"

CHAPTER SIX

One, in their right mind, might think Katelyn's gratitude for that dreadful night nineteen years ago was a bit deranged. Weird. Scary even. Who, in their right mind, would be thankful for coming face to face with a demon? Certainly not any normal human...right? Then again, Katelyn was far from being what the world considered normal. Her life never fit the role of the humdrum, take it one day at a time, living for the moment lifestyle that seemed to fill the void of everyone else's entire existence. No. That was never enough for her.

She yearned for adventure. For a family, though hers was a far cry from the loving one she'd always envisioned herself growing up in. For relationships, she could count on no matter how dark the days became.

It was unfortunate that only one person met that definition in her life, back then. And it was also sad that that particular person was no longer on this side of eternity. There would be no chance to tell her Aunt Cara about the love of Jesus. No opportunity to show her a different version of life. No chance to actually love her unconditionally...though she thought she did at the time. Boy, had she been mistaken.

The realization of her love being a cheaper, lesser version of all it could've been, saddened Katelyn at times. She often wondered how they were both so blind to the deceit, to the hatred. Blind to the confusion and fear that had ruled their lives. Though maybe her aunt hadn't been blind to it all? Perhaps she had fed off all the negative energy?

Wondering about the darkness that controlled and overran Cara's heart would've consumed Katelyn if she'd let it. Instead, she learned to turn her thoughts to the decision she had chosen that night long ago.

The decision to walk in freedom. Freedom of fear. Freedom of guilt. Freedom of sadness. Freedom of all of the lies she had ever believed. Not only about herself...but about God. About love, about life.

It was there, in those moments...in those thoughts that a renewed sense of worth, of belief, had taken her over. For that, she would always be thankful. For that, she would gladly go through it all again. How could she not?

Had things turned out any other way, she probably wouldn't be where she was today. Holding onto bitterness and anger was futile. Those emotions would only bring self-destruction, and finding out there was so much more to live for was well worth laying it all down.

"Hey, Katelyn, honey, what time are we supposed to pick up, Celeste?" She vaguely heard Trevor's voice but didn't respond, lost too much in her own thoughts.

"Katelyn, everything all right?" A strong yet gentle warmth rested on her shoulder. She raised her arm and placed her hand over her husband's. "Yeah," she smiled, "everything is fine." She glanced at the clock. "Pretty sure we were supposed to be there already."

Trevor squeezed her shoulder, "We should probably get going then."

"Yes, we should. Time got away from me again. I'll call and let her know we're running behind."

"Sounds good. I'll wait for you in the car."

"I'll be down in a minute."

Katelyn dialed Celeste's number. Three rings and her daughter's voice was on the other end, "Hello?"

"Hey, dad and I are running behind, we're leaving the house now."

"Yeah, okay. See you soon."

Before Katelyn could say anything else, Celeste ended the call. Katelyn stared at her phone and tried to shake off the uneasy feeling that crept in around her. She placed her phone in her purse and grabbed the house keys.

In no time at all, Trevor and Katelyn had pulled up in front of Stacey's house. Trevor pushed down on the middle of the wheel, and an annoying noise briefly filled the air.

Katelyn looked at her watch. Too many minutes had passed. "I'm going to go get her," Katelyn said as she opened the car door. "Be right back."

One knock later and a worried Stacey along with her mother stood next to a parked car and two perplexed and concerned parents.

How can this be happening? A million scenarios flashed through Katelyn's mind. She watched as Trevor dialed Celeste's number for the third time. Their daughter wasn't where she was supposed to be. There had been no school project. The past month had been a lie.

A shiver ran through Katelyn and caused the fine hairs along her arms to stand on end. Her heart beat faster. Something was wrong. She sensed it now. Sensed the despair, the heaviness in the air as it blew against her, weighing her down. *Lord, how did I miss this?*

"She's not answering, Katelyn."

Katelyn stood shaking as she watched Trevor in what seemed like slow motion make his way over to her. Strong arms wrapped around her, pulling her trembling body next to his. Her head moved slightly up and down with every breath Trevor took.

Katelyn tried to push the gulp in her throat back down, but it fought relentlessly to be released. Finally, it won. Tears dampened her cheeks. Her insides trembled. "Trevor, I don't have a good feeling about this. I haven't felt like this in a long time."

"It'll be all right. We'll find Celeste."

Nothing Trevor said or could say, would lessen the awful feeling. It was not possible. The last time this kind of unease pressed this heavily against her soul had been years ago.

"They're back, Trevor. They're after our daughter."

It was at that moment a dark figure came walking out of the shadows. "Mom, Dad?"

"Celes-," Katelyn started to speak but quieted at the shake of her husband's head. "Get in the car, Celeste."

It was strange; the fear that mingled with the authority in Trevor's tone. It had been so long since Katelyn heard a quiver in his baritone voice. It caught her off guard. *Lord, help us.*

Katelyn knew now where all the restlessness came from. Internally she chastised herself for not seeing the signs sooner. As much as she disliked her daughter being the enemy's target, there was a little sliver of peace deep down inside that was thankful she finally had a direction to pray in.

It was just the beginning, that was the cold hard truth of the matter, but being able to rest in the One that held the ending ignited a fire inside. One the enemy would be sorry was ever re-lit.

CHAPTER SEVEN

Other than a sigh and the occasional humph from the backseat, the ride home was a relatively quiet one. It gave Trevor time to think things over and pray before the confrontation that was coming. He pulled in the drive and placed the car in park before shutting it off. Trevor followed Katelyn and Celeste into the house then shut the door behind them. He prayed God would give him the strength to remain calm.

"What were you thinking, Celeste? We were worried sick about you."

"Sorry, Dad. I just wanted to be with my friend. I guess you wouldn't understand how that feels though, right?"

His daughter's sarcastically laced response caught him off guard. This young woman wasn't the same person who'd left his presence a couple hours ago. Could so much really change in such a short amount of time? Katelyn had to be right, he determined. They'd missed something somewhere.

"You know we do, so where is all this coming from? What's going on?" Katelyn asked. Celeste crossed her arms. A small smirk rested on her lips. "Why, mother, whatever do you mean? I'm a perfectly normal hormonal girl, just testing my boundaries."

"What?" Katelyn answered.

Trevor started to say something but stopped at the nod of Katelyn's head. "I'll give you two some time to talk," he said instead.

"What's the matter, Dad, can't take the heat?"

Trevor stopped and faced his daughter. He looked her in the eyes. He didn't like what stared back at him.

Emptiness.

He shook his head and gathered his thoughts. "Celeste, I love you. You are my only child. I adore you and want only the best for you. That's all I've ever wanted, for all of us. So your disobedience to us, to God, weighs heavily on my heart. Your mother and I do not want to see you go down the wrong path. There's too much at stake. Your life is too important. Maybe you're too young to fully understand what that means, I don't know? But you were entrusted into our care. I hope you come to realize that we do what we think is best for you."

"Trev, let me talk with her for a little while."

"Yeah, sure." He turned and continued in his original direction. Defeat carved itself in the deep, bunched up lines between his brows, and he started to pray, "I need Your guidance, Lord. Even if I don't like them, I need answers. I don't know if my words got through to her, Lord. From the look of hate in her eyes, I doubt it.

The backdoor rubbed against the welcome mat as he pushed it open. "What do I do?" he whispered. "And Katelyn's feeling earlier. That look on her face." He sighed. "Where did my little girl go? The one that used to sit on my lap and read me stories. The one that wanted me to kiss every scratch. The one who trusted me with all her secrets? Where did she go?"

"She's still there," came a whisper.

Tension, the arrogant demon he was, filled the room with his dark and wispy mist. It concealed his body and left only his red, beady eyes to be seen. Eyes that quickly darted back and forth between the two humans in front of him. He was good at causing trouble, and that's what he'd come here to do. He whispered something into Celeste's ear. A sinister grin parted his thick, cracked lips, just enough to reveal the sharp points of his teeth, and he waited to see the look on the face of the young puppet's parent.

A squeal of laughter cut through the fog, leaving a clear space to linger for a moment before coming back together. This mission would be an entertaining one.

Uneasiness and peace fought for the starring role in Katelyn's own insider film. She knew now, without a doubt, what filled her house. What was at work in her daughter's life. Several times she'd unknowingly looked through the lanky demon across the room from her. And more than several times an old familiar tingle ran across her shoulders. She patted the empty place next to her on the couch. "Come, sit down."

"Why? So you can drill me with all the same stuff dad just did?"

"No, not exactly the same."

"Great."

"Celeste, you do know what you did was wrong, don't you?"

Celeste grumbled through gritted teeth. "Why? Why is wanting to spend time with my friend wrong?"

Katelyn sighed. Everything about the present situation

sent warning bells blasting off inside her. Had it really been almost twenty years since she'd had a very similar conversation with her parents?

"There's nothing wrong with hanging out with friends. Your father and I both want you to be able to do that. To go and spend time with others and build lasting relationships. But when you feel you have to lie about it and hide it... honey, that's a whole other story. That has us concerned for you and your well being."

"You just don't understand! He's not a bad person!"

Katelyn wished she didn't understand. She'd prayed for an open and honest relationship with her daughter for years. One that was so very different than that of hers with her own mom. Her nerves tingled, every one of her senses on high alert. "Wait, you were with a boy tonight?"

"Yes."

"Were you alone?"

"Yes, we were alone."

Images ran through Katelyn's mind, turning her stomach.

"Don't worry, Mom. Nothing happened. You made sure of that."

"How do you mean?"

"May I go now? It's late, and I'm tired."

Katelyn glanced at the clock on the DVD player across the room. "You're right. It is late. But I think there's still a little more we need to talk about."

"Like what?"

"Well, why don't you start at the beginning. What happened that made you think this behavior is okay?"

Celeste's narrowed eyes stared in her Mother's direction. "I don't want to talk about it."

"I get that. But we need to. I can't help you unless you talk to me. Unless you are honest with me."

"Honest, huh," Celeste laughed, "honesty is important to you, is it?"

"Of course it is. You know that."

"Well, mom, to me, keeping secrets is not being very honest, is it?"

Katelyn was shocked by her daughter's accusation, though she tried to not let it show. She and Trevor had always been as open about things as they could. Katelyn searched through her memories for something she may have kept hidden; something other than that night so long ago. Surely her daughter wasn't referring to that? How could she even know about that anyway? Ultimately, though, she came up empty. "What have I not been honest about, Celeste?"

"Funny you're the one asking me that question. You know what, maybe we should just calm down. Sleep on things and start over in the morning. What do you say?" Celeste said with a sneer.

Katelyn leaned back under the frightful force of Celeste's words. She grabbed the armrest next to her, now fully aware of the secret her daughter was talking about. "Those words," she whispered, "my words. How?"

"Pretty much your exact words, if I'm correct. And I'm sure the how will come out in due time."

Nothing more was said.

"I'm going to bed now."

Katelyn sighed and watched her daughter walk away. "How does she know?" she questioned.

CHAPTER EIGHT

Two figures, massive in size, took up almost the entire space of Celeste's room. Matching grins had crept over their thin, charcoal lips, revealing the jagged points of yellow stained teeth. "See, Ackmen. I told you there would come a time when a door would be opened, and we'd be right there, waiting." The yellow mist from Melti's breath filled the air, coating everything around them with a cloud of putrid pixie-dust-like substance.

"She's not a Burnsten."

"Not fully, no, but the Burnsten blood runs through her veins nonetheless. Curiosity, at this age, is such a fun thing to play with."

"Katelyn's response to her own words echoed back at her was priceless," Ackmen cackled.

"Yes, we must be careful now. Katelyn will know we're back. Her prayers will most certainly call on a war."

"Necklim?" Ackmen questioned.

"I wouldn't doubt it," Melti answered.

"Great, just who I want to see."

"Your quivering tone says otherwise. No confident demon should shudder at the name of an angel."

"I don't like him, Melti. You know that," Ackmen hissed.

"None of us do."

"His threats," Ackmen interjected.

"Have remained unfulfilled," Melti responded.

"For now."

"Ackmen, do you not believe in your ability to win in a battle against the puny angel?"

Melti's sarcastic impression didn't go by unnoticed. He could tell by the look on the low-ranking demon beside him. Weakness.

"I do."

"You should. Necklim got lucky when he took out Latar. We won't give him that chance again."

Ackmen joined with Melti and directed his stare in the young girl's direction. There was no sense in worrying about what might happen. There was no time for that.

The anger inside Celeste grew like the flames of a fire being slowly stoked. It dulled her judgment. Her senses. There was no uneasiness at the demons' unseen stares drilling into her; instead, the hate intensified, fueled by the overwhelming surge of power. Her words had struck a nerve, the look on her mom's face had said as much. "Honesty, huh? Important? Right." The sting of betrayal was a hurtful one. Why had her mom kept so much from her? Her whole childhood felt like a lie. All the open lines of communication seemed to only flow in one direction. Or did it?

She knew she should tell her mom about the book, about the note she'd found inside. But would she? Could she? What would her mom think? What would she do? Celeste no longer trusted herself to do the right thing, how would her mom be able to?

"Humph, honesty is for the weak," she whispered in anger.

A part of her recoiled at the unfamiliar words that slipped through her lips. This wasn't how she was raised. Wasn't how she spoke, believed. Was it? Maybe it was now. A lot had changed since meeting Daren. It wasn't long before the hatred and distrust buried the guilt deep within.

Trevor looked at his wife sitting on the couch. He could only imagine what happened between her and their daughter. From the look on her face, it couldn't have been anything good. She seemed lost in her thoughts. He didn't want to scare her, so he whispered her name as he came up behind and placed his hands on her shoulders. He gave them a slight squeeze and asked, "Everything alright?" though he already knew the answer.

"No, not really."

"What happened?"

Katelyn blinked several times before noticing Trevor was now in front of her. She tilted her head up in his direction, and said, "She knows."

Confusion played with the lines on Trevor's face. "She knows? Knows what?"

"I think she knows everything."

"What did she say?"

"The same exact words I said to my parents before my mom left us that night. How did she know what I said, Trevor? How?"

Trevor shook his head. "I don't know. Maybe she overheard us talking about it?"

"We've never talked about that around her."

"I know. I don't have an answer."

"Maybe mom slipped and said something to her?"

"You could ask her, Katelyn, but honestly, I don't think she would do that."

"I don't either. But I'm at a loss here, Trevor."

Trevor wrapped Katelyn's hands in his own and knelt down in front her. "Everything will be okay. We'll get through this."

"I know. It's just the last thing I expected to hear from Celeste, you know?"

He raised her hand to his lips and gently kissed the tops of her fingers. "I know. But none of this has taken God by surprise, right?"

"Right."

"Let's pray," Trevor said, and they both closed their eyes.

Celeste's room was quiet. Darkness had extinguished the pale slivers of moonlight that had covered the far bedroom wall. Melti's gruesome voice flowed through the pitch black space and entered into the innermost part of Celeste's mind. The places of things unseen and unknown to anyone except the repulsive figures that stood next to her. They whispered plans of danger, hatred, and backlash. They whispered of lies and deceit. Minute after minute, hour after hour, these deep voices entangled themselves around the truth, choking it out completely. Growing in intensity and in strength, they knocked out what very little faith Celeste had left.

Melti glanced up and noticed the night had started to give way to the light. "The sun will rise soon. Our part is done for tonight," he said. "We will return in due time."

Melti and Ackmen disappeared through the roof and blended in with the shadowy darkness of the pre-dawn sky above the house. The evil look of pleasure on their faces matched the disdain inside their hideous forms. A sudden movement on the reasonably concealed ground below caused them to stop and look more closely. A small form sat on a whitewashed bench, encircled by yellow, pink, and purple flowers. A Bible laid open on its lap.

"Who does she think she is?" Ackmen questioned as they landed in front of her, watching as her light pink lips silently moved.

"Apparently she has too much faith in her God and His angels. They will not win again." Melti snickered and rose to his full height, sticking out his chest while his thin, tattered, leathery wings unfolded behind him. He was a mortifying sight to see. One that would easily cause a faint heart to stop beating.

Katelyn finished her prayers just before the sun began to rise. She slowly opened her eyes, picked up the Bible from her lap, and stood. Her green eyes met the glowing red ones that were feet above her. Boldness started to flow from deep within until it reached every last area of her body. Then she spoke, unafraid of the evilness in front of her, and answered Ackmen's question. "I'll tell you who I *know* I am. I am a child of the King. Who do you *think* you are?"

Melti and Ackmen were knocked back several steps from the authority in Katelyn's words. A sudden sense of dread from a previous defeat crept around them. Their arrogant smugness had been taken down a few notches, but they wouldn't let that stop them. The plan for Celeste was in place, and this time they wouldn't allow anything to stand in their way.

Katelyn waved her finger back and forth between the two charcoal-colored giants in front of her. She ended their brief encounter with three little words. "This. Means. War."

CHAPTER NINE

Necklim had told the Commander of everything he'd heard and felt on his visit to the Holcomb's. After receiving the mission, he quickly left the Throne Room and headed for the golden horn that hung from a long silver rope off the front of the main palace. He blew it a total of ten times – once for each Warrior he'd need with him. Though he had a feeling that wouldn't be the final count.

He listened as the low baritone sound vibrated the airwaves throughout the heavenly realm, reaching to every last corner, alerting all Warriors of the coming battle.

One by one, the Warriors landed before him. His faithful friends and comrades were the first to appear. Denab, Nolan, Sarta, Ezera touched down in front of him at almost the same time. Soon followed by Nisha, Kanu, Layden, Reneese, Malkia, and Nalof.

"Some of you have fought bravely by my side against these particular demons before," Necklim began, he looked from Sarta to Ezera then from Denab to Nolan, "and some of you have not. Those of you who haven't will be working alongside those of us who have. No demon should be taken lightly, but these are some of the highest-ranking demons under the father of lies himself. We must work together. We must be alert." Necklim looked over his fellow fighters as they nodded their understanding. "Good, if everyone is ready I'll place you in teams and give you your charges and posts." The fighters nodded in agreement.

"Denab, you and Nisha will watch over those who were part of the previous battle with Katelyn several years ago, Miranda and her husband, Jeremy. Go with them wherever they go. Sarta, you and Kanu, will stand guard over Katelyn and Trevor's parents. Ezera, you and Layden, will be over the Holcomb's church family. You're not required to stand guard over any particular person but the local church. You are to go back and forth between them all. If there comes a time when this task becomes too much for you, let me know, and I'll call for more Warriors. I don't foresee Melti coming against the church body, at least not at first. In my past experience, he goes after those closest to the person he is seeking out. Does that mean he won't? No. But this is plan A. Any questions, so far?"

Necklim took a breather and waited a few moments before he continued. "Nolan, Reneese, Malkia, and Nalof, you four will be with me at the Holcomb's residence. We will guard Katelyn, Trevor, and Celeste. I don't know yet how close we will be able to get to Celeste, but our presence in the house will be recognized before nightfall. This is bound to stir up some things. Melti is sly, so be watchful and ever ready."

Necklim pulled his sword from his sheath, and the others followed suit. The swords gave off a bright light that sparkled like the night stars as their tips were touched. "For the Worthy!" They called out in unison.

Kanone stood behind Katelyn. His unfolded wings slightly wrapped around her. He had witnessed the exchange of words between his charge and the demons. Things were getting worse. Melti's and Ackmen's presence confirmed that. "What right do they have to come against my daughter? Didn't they learn from the first go around that they won't win?" he heard Katelyn whisper.

"Of course not. Maybe the demons are not afraid. Well, guess what," Katelyn said looking towards the sky, "This time, I'm not afraid."

Kanone had come to appreciate Katelyn's tenacity. He smiled at the confident woman she'd become. If anyone in that home was ready for the fight soon to take place, she was, and Kanone was not the only one who knew that. Nove, Trevor's Guardian, had spoken of Katelyn's growth in the Lord over the years as well.

"If only more would choose to be like you, Katelyn. The world just might be a better place." Kanone's words were unheard and carried away with the wind. This he knew, but he couldn't help but speak the truth.

Katelyn started towards the house, and Kanone followed, walking through the door that had been closed in front of him. The woman knelt at the couch. Hushed tones, barely audible to the human ear, were loud and clear in his own. He took a breath, soaked in the moment and then let his worship mingle with the that of the beautiful soul in front of him. Their praises intertwined and filled the small room before seeping up through the roof and towards Heaven.

The calm before the storm had finally broke, and the smell of war filled the air. If history proved itself right, yet again, then that's definitely what was on the horizon. Kanone expected to see Warrior Angels and soon.

Tensions ran high in the confines of a damp, dark cave. Angry voices bellowed and echoed throughout the maze that was the demons' home base for the small town of Green Hill, Kentucky. Melti shook his fist and brought it down with such force on the table in front of him that it broke apart and sent tiny shards of splintered wood flying through the air. His encounter with Katelyn had gotten the best of him. Struck a sense of fear in the demon's core that hadn't been dealt with in quite some time.

Ackmen's eyes met with Melti's. "We are no longer after Katelyn. We are after her daughter."

"Who said we were finished with Katelyn?" Melti growled.

"I just assumed."

Melti cut him off, "You assumed wrong."

"After all these years you are going to try and win her over?"

"I don't see why not."

"Melti, surely you, the head demon, can see that fight would be a lost cause. Katelyn Holcomb, turning her back on her beliefs? I don't see it happening."

Melti positioned his sharply tipped appendage on the edge of Ackmen's pointy nose. "Then it's a good thing you are not in charge, isn't it?"

Ackmen refused to answer. Once Melti set his twisted mind on doing something, it would be done. His hatred towards Katelyn had grown so intense over the years, Ackmen knew there was no stopping him. He did wonder how this would affect their stance with Celeste. Wasting precious time on Katelyn could possibly weaken their hold on the daughter. From past experiences, Ackmen knew a little

50

window was all those pesky Warriors needed to slip in and turn a winning battle into a mighty defeat.

All Ackmen could do, if he wanted to keep his head attached to his muscled-covered shoulders, was shake it off and let Melti have his way. Despite how wrong that way may be. "Fine, Melti," Ackmen's words slithered through the air like that of a hissing snake. "You win. We will go after them both."

Melti grinned. "I know we will."

CHAPTER TEN

Necklim's white, feathery wings folded up behind him as he came to a soft landing on the Holcomb's front lawn. Rays of the morning sun filtered through the leaves of the tall oak trees and danced across the front of the house with the light breeze. Memories filled his thoughts. The secret hope of the demon's obsession with Katelyn and her family ending with Latar was now nonexistent. The twisted schemes were not sent to the pit along with him.

Necklim stepped onto the drive. The gravel rearranged under his feet. "Are you ready?" he asked of those with him. Not turning to see their answers, he remained facing the structure that housed his charges and waited to hear confident voices of acceptance.

"Yes!" The Warriors shouted in unison.

"Go then, guard your charges," Necklim said.

"Shall we enter with you?" Nolan asked, coming to stand at Necklim's side.

"Yes." Necklim turned towards the angels left with him. "We will enter together, united, through the front door, then make our way throughout each room in the home. We need to find out where our boundaries are."

"There are Guardians here. Will they be staying as well, Necklim?" Reneese asked.

Necklim gave Reneese his attention. "They will. Though they will not be taking part in the battle." Reneese nodded.

"Let's go, then." Necklim stepped through the closed door, his fellow Warriors close behind. Celeste's room was the last door on the right. All the house, but this room, would be entirely their territory.

The Warriors stopped in front of the door where they held little ground. The enemy was more than likely on the other side, but that hindered not their entrance. The sensation of betrayal met them like a slap in the face. It was strong. Powerful. Fresh.

Necklim scanned Celeste's room, his gaze finally stopping on a crinkled piece of paper on the floor. He picked it up. "This is how Celeste found out everything." He turned and handed it to Nolan. "I have no doubt where it came from, but my suspicions must be confirmed."

"Agreed."

"Nolan, I want you to follow Celeste. Though our presence is now known to the enemy, I want you to keep concealed for the time being."

"Of course."

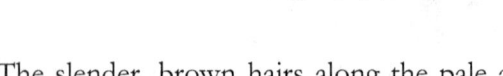

The slender, brown hairs along the pale arms of the girl on the bed stood on end as the paper she'd wadded up and thrown on the floor the night before began to move on its own. Celeste didn't believe in ghosts. Angels and demons, however, now that was a different story. Which of these beings had moved the paper was unknown at the moment, and she wasn't sure she really wanted to know. There were no, what one might call, creepy feelings, but no pleasant ones either. Forgetting the scene in front of her and going back to texting Daren like nothing had ever happened was highly unlikely. Once something was seen it can't be unseen, or at least that's what they say. Figuring out if that statement was true was next on the agenda.

The vibration of her phone distracted her from the unexplained and brought her focus back to the small screen now held tightly in her hand. After responding to Daren's text, she placed the phone on the nightstand and decided it was time to get away from whatever was occupying the same space as herself and end the constant growling and groaning noises coming from her stomach.

A warmth met her hand as she reached for the doorknob. Such a contrast to the cold isolation she felt moments before. She pulled back. The heat was gone, only to be felt once again just mere inches from the door. She looked around. Nothing could be seen that would explain the difference in temperature. No window was open, or fan going. *Okay, strange. All the more reason to get out of here.*

She pushed through the warmth and opened the door. Seconds later and Celeste was looking over her shoulder, shaking her head in denial. This was too much. Good or evil, Celeste didn't want anything to do with it.

"Weird feeling, isn't it?"

Katelyn's voice startled Celeste. She stumbled, catching herself on the wall. "What?" she asked in disgust.

"Sorry, I didn't mean to scare you."

"You didn't scare me, and I don't know what you're talking about. I thought I heard my phone so I turned around."

"Oh, okay then." Her mom had not even tried to hide the fact she didn't believe her. Celeste walked by pretending like it didn't bother her one way or another. Though they both knew otherwise. For the most part, Celeste was a lot like her mom. Headstrong at times, maybe, but usually full of grace and forgiveness. A heart of empathy beat within her chest. At least it used to. Anymore she wasn't so sure.

"I'm sure you're hungry," Katelyn continued, "it's well past noon. Would you like me to make you something to eat?"

"No. I got it."

"We need to talk, Celeste. Maybe after you've got some food in you, we could go out and sit in the garden?"

"You know, I'm not sure. I think I'm pretty busy all day."

"Celeste?"

"Why aren't you at church, anyway? I thought there was a picnic or something after service today?"

"We stayed home today, so we could sort all this out, or attempt to at least."

"Wow, missing church...because of me? Careful, Mom, people might start to talk."

"So be it, if they must, but I don't think talking is what they'll be doing. Praying is more like it."

The opened jug of milk in Celeste's hand slammed onto the counter spraying small droplets of its contents on her fingers. *How could she?* "I can't believe this! You told them, didn't you?"

"Watch your tone with me, young lady. And no, I didn't tell anyone anything. I did, however, ask Miranda and Jeremy for their prayers."

"Great, mom. Everyone will know it was because of me."

"Why do you say that?"

"You've never missed a service as far as I can remember. What do you think everyone is going to think when you don't show up after finding out your precious daughter lied the night before?"

"If anyone knows of what happened last night it's not

because of me or your dad. People can think and say what they will. My concern is not with them. It is however with you."

Celeste poured the milk over her cereal before sitting down at the table. Things had definitely changed. Life, in all of its wonderful amazement, had a funny way of rearranging thoughts and priorities that one once held so dear, and smashing them like a glass bottle on the floor. So many tiny, sharp pieces. So easily able to nick the skin, revealing how fragile it really is. Exposing what's hidden underneath to the cold and cruel elements of its surroundings.

Yeah, life...it had definitely changed.

CHAPTER ELEVEN

Deception couldn't believe what he felt, though it was not something one could easily forget. When the enemy had been in your territory, there was a recognizable charge, a difference that permeated the air. An essence only heavenly beings omitted.

It was that essence that had invaded their well-earned space. Melti was not going to be happy. Though the Warriors arrival was expected, it wasn't expected so soon. They were not ready. The early presence of the enemy was no doubt thanks to the meddling Guardians. They were an added bother this time around that hadn't had to be addressed with Katelyn.9Voices down the hall caught Deception's attention. He floated towards them, leary of which Warrior he'd find. To his surprise, it was only the two humans. "I know you're here, Warrior. I can feel you. Show yourself!"

Nothing materialized. Not being able to see your enemy was never a good feeling. "Fine. You just wait until Melti shows up," he hissed, then went over to Celeste, stopping with his mouth mere centimeters from her ear. He whispered his twisted questions and accusations as quietly as possible, hoping that against all odds the enemy wouldn't hear. Would Melti understand? Probably not. What choice was there? Showing up before Melti with loose ends, no way. That was never done. The chance had to be taken.

A searing, powerful warmth overtook him and completely severed what little concentration he had.

"Back off, Warrior! She's ours now." Deception sneered.

He took in the room around him, slowly turning to scan every nook and cranny for any sort of response. He knew the Warriors were close for the heat stayed on him, increasing ever so slightly with each tick-tock of the clock.

Deception went back to business until he could no longer handle the heavenly fire bearing down on him. Back up would be needed to keep this running smoothly, and Melti's approval would be required before that could happen.

Deception snarled through his teeth. Showing up before Melti, uninvited, didn't always turn out so well.

"What's the meaning of your interruption, Deception?" Melti yelled. The vibration loosened tiny bits of debris from the cave walls and sent them scattering to the floor.

"My, lord. The enemy has arrived."

"Already? This wasn't expected yet."

"Their presence is strong, my lord. I will need back up to stay on track."

"So be it. We can't deviate from our plan," Melti growled. "Ackmen, go with Deception. Don't let those vile hosts of heaven anywhere near Deception or Celeste."

"GO!"

Melti paced back and forth. The confines of the tiny space only made his temper flare more. His clawed hand dug into the hard cave wall beside him. He couldn't let the Warriors arrival distract him.

His eyes narrowed. His breath increased. His heart

thumped against his chest. Tonight he would put an end to what stood in his way. He would rule the heart of his target. No light from above would stop him.

His strength had increased throughout the years. His wisdom had grown. He'd watched in silent anticipation for this very moment in time. Calculated every twist and turn to make this happen. Every lie that would chip away at the girls faith. Every hurt that would stay engraved in her heart. Every word that would snake its way through her core. Every friction that would be everlasting. This was his time. She was his trophy. He would not let her go without a fight. Even if it meant losing his subjects in battle.

Who were they to him anyway? They were lucky to be in his presence. Lucky to be called to such a great mission. He would not fail. Let his enemies bring the fight. He would end it.

<hr />

Katelyn waited while Celeste placed her bowl in the sink, watching each slow and deliberate move she'd made. Celeste was not in the mood to talk, that much was clear. But it must be done. Things had to be aired out. Never in a million years had Katelyn thought Celeste would take those secrets to heart like she had.

They weren't meant for her ears just yet. It wasn't that she had never intended to inform Celeste, she only hadn't been sure when. Age, maturity, a better understanding of what it all entailed was required before opening and exposing those parts of her life...of their family. *Maybe I still see her too much as a child?*

Katelyn was sure Celeste had felt something in the hall earlier, though she would never admit it. Was she ready?

Time would soon tell.

When Celeste hadn't moved from the sink, Katelyn walked over and carefully placed her hand on her daughter's shoulder. Muscles tensed. Katelyn pulled her hand away, not wanting to put any more of a strain on their relationship than there was already. Katelyn's struggles with her parents had taught her to approach things lightly, gently, when it came to someone who felt betrayed.

"Cee, will you please talk to me? I will tell you everything. I will answer any questions you have. Please just give me a chance to explain."

Silence.

Even the breaths between them couldn't be heard. Celeste had opened her mouth slightly, only to close it before saying anything. Katelyn tried again. "Why don't we start with you asking me whatever is on your mind? Once I've answered, I'll ask you something. Can we at least start there?"

Seconds passed, though it felt more like an eternity to Katelyn. She held her breathe, only to release it when she heard Celeste finally say something.

"Okay, Mom."

Katelyn smiled. It was more than she'd hoped for, so she'd take it. "Whenever you're ready."

"I've lied to you, Mom. In fact, I've been lying to you for months now. Do you still love me?"

Celeste's question took Katelyn by surprise. Did her precious daughter honestly think lying would cause them not to love her? She couldn't really believe that, could she?

"Oh, Celeste. Yes. I still love you. Dad still loves you. Most importantly, God still loves you. Actions, they don't change the way a parent feels towards their child. Just as they don't change the way, God feels towards His children. It doesn't mean that the lies don't hurt, or that I agree with it. But I will always love you."

Celeste looked towards the floor. "I guess it's your turn now."

Katelyn wasn't sure where to start. So many questions swirled in her mind. Finally, she decided to stick with her daughters line of questioning. "I've kept some things from you, though it was for a reason maybe, I should have told you there were things we'd need to talk about one day. One day when you were older and could understand better. So, do you still love me?"

Shock replaced Celeste's sorrow-filled features. Katelyn could tell she hadn't expected that.

"Yes, Mom. I still love you. It doesn't mean it doesn't hurt though. Finding things out from a piece of paper that just so happened to fall out of an ancient, messed up bo – ," Celeste stopped. "Ancient book? What ancient book?" Katelyn questioned after Celeste went quiet.

"Never mind that. Besides it's my turn to ask a question, remember?"

CHAPTER TWELVE

Katelyn and Celeste stood in the kitchen, encircled under the protective shield of Necklim's and Nolan's wings. The Warriors were thankful to have gotten rid of Deception, at least for a little while. This time was needed. Mending between mom and daughter had to begin. The Warriors weren't sure how much time Deception's absence would buy them, so they wasted none of the precious seconds given and sent gentle nudges in Katelyn's direction. When she glanced up, Necklim saw the hope come alive in her. Though they wouldn't show themselves just yet, they knew their message had been received.

"Yes, you're correct. It is your turn." Katelyn smiled at her daughter, hoping to keep this going as long as possible. Time, she knew, it was more than likely not on her side. Any moments allotted to her with her daughter wouldn't be wasted. They couldn't be.

"Honestly, Mom, I don't even know where to start. You already said you hadn't brought it up because of my age. Which, from some of the stuff I read, I guess I can understand why. It's a lot. Weird."

"It was. It is," Katelyn agreed.

"You loved your Aunt Cara, a lot...didn't you?"

"I did. At that time in my life, I felt she was the only one who understood me. Turns out, it was all just an act. She told me what I wanted to hear in hopes of bringing me into something I had no idea about...something I didn't even know existed. It was hard to learn the truth. Scary. The evil I faced...I wouldn't wish that on anyone."

"What got you through it?"

Katelyn smiled. "Holy Warriors. Angels meant for battle that had been sent by God. They fought for me. They let me know I was worthy."

"Do you think everyone has Warrior Angels looking for out for them?"

"When the need for them arises, yes, I do."

"Did, Cara?"

"She did. She chose not to accept the call, not to hear of God's love."

"That's sad."

"It is. I wish Cara would've. Sometimes though, lies, deceit, betrayal, guilt...well they can make you do things you normally wouldn't. Ya, know?"

Katelyn knew there was something Celeste wanted to tell her by the way she diverted her eyes. A great deal of sadness...regret seemed to wash over her daughter. She prayed for time to stand still, for Celeste to have courage, for trust to be there. For her daughter to open up.

"Mom?"

"Yes."

Celeste's voice was a whisper. "I almost did something. Something I know is wrong. I'm sorry."

Katelyn wiped the tears from her daughter's cheeks and wrapped her tightly in her arms. "No one makes the right choices all the time. Our feelings can take us down paths we'd never thought we'd go if we're not careful."

"Nothing like learning that the hard way."

"Celeste, life is a never-ending lesson." Katelyn chuckled. "I think you're right, Mom."

Necklim took notice at the change in temperature around them. A demon now occupied the space behind him – more hideous and crafty than Deception could ever dare dream to be.

"Ackmen," Necklim whispered, his one brow raised. "This should be fun."

Nolan's laugh filled the protective cocoon they'd formed around Katelyn and Celeste.

"Deception's back up, I'm sure. How much time do you think we have before he returns?"

"Not long. We need to let Katelyn know. Once he arrives, I'm afraid this moment will be gone. Deception, though a spirit, is good at what he does."

"I agree."

Necklim placed his strong hand on Katelyn's shoulder and whispered in her ear, his warning only leaving them mere seconds. "Be ready, Katelyn. Ackmen has returned."

Katelyn shivered at Necklim's warning. She didn't want to let go of her daughter. Didn't want to lose this connection with her. It was just starting. She held onto her daughter a little tighter and confirmed their love...God's love for her. "Baby," she held Celeste's face, hands shaking, "no matter what happens, no matter what choices you make or don't make, know that your Dad and I love you, and we'll always be here for you. Seek the truth in everything. Know to whom you belong. Don't be easily deceived."

Ackmen snarled at the heavenly presence surrounding his target. There was more than one Warrior in that kitchen. The odds of Necklim being one had his insides slightly fluttering, and the fact that they didn't reveal themselves when he'd appeared only added to his aggravation. "Remove your protective shield!" Ackmen ordered. "The girl is our target. You have lost too much ground to be guarding her like you are!" his gravelly voice bellowed.

A warmth that could only come from Heaven moved away from the two girls standing near the sink.

Ackmen didn't like the looks of what had been happening under the shield of the angels. Celeste's face was a bit more peaceful, hopeful even. That would have to change, and quick. Melti couldn't know how far the two had come in the few short minutes that Deception was gone.

He was in a foul enough mood already. Wanting to take on both girls in this house, what was he thinking? It was a joke. It would never happen. They'd never have the one girl and stood a good chance at losing the other if they didn't watch what they were doing.

Melti's greed, his bruised ego couldn't take the hit from Katelyn. It had him reckless. They couldn't afford to be careless...not now.

"Deception, to your post." Ackmen pointed to the young girl in front of them.

Deception hovered just above her head and started the attack.

Ackmen could see the questioning start to come back in the way Celeste held her head, in the look in her eyes. It was working. Good.

"You know, Mom, I think I'm going to go back to my room now. I have some things I need to do."

"Okay, Cee. I'm here if you need me."

Ackmen hung around and waited to see the defeat take control of Katelyn. It didn't. He moved closer to her, aiming to strike a blow of his own. One that would start a tidal wave of frustration and hopelessness, growing and festering until her guard was down. Even if it was a small break, it would be one they could work their way through. He lunged at her, hands before him ready to sink his talons deep into her mind, but stopped at the bright, solid figure of pure strength in his path. A warm glow shot out, striking Ackmen in the chest. He winced, shook it off and moved towards Katelyn once more.

A jab, to his right shoulder, stopped his advances yet again.

"That's enough, Ackmen."

Ackmen's muscular legs wobbled briefly. *Why me? Why him?* "Necklim?"

The blonde headed angel's body of stone appeared before him, sword in hand. "The one and only."

CHAPTER THIRTEEN

Celeste closed the door behind her and leaned up against it. Why she'd told her mom what she had was beyond her. What was she thinking? Opening up, after all this? It had felt good, though. A reprieve. A pouring out of one's self. It had been freeing, as much as she hated to admit it.

She couldn't let it happen again. Her mom's words...they had to be lies, right? They tumbled in her thoughts and mixed with her emotions. "She can't love me anymore. I'm such a screw-up! She only said that because she doesn't know what I almost did. What would she think of me then? Her precious daughter in the arms of a boy? How'd I let myself come so far, get in this deep?"

◆ ◆ ◆ ◆

Deception twirled his snaky finger over Celeste's head. Hopelessness began to cloud Celeste's judgment. Stopped her rational thinking. "Yes, dear girl. How could she possibly love you? There's no way," he whispered in her ear.

The tears streaming down her face brought joy to his morbid soul. Lies were his strong suit. It was what he was all about. Making a human miserable was his specialty. Most could be swayed, deceived, with hardly any effort. It was too easy really. Celeste was too easy. He'd expected more of a struggle from this girl. Katelyn was her mom after all. Maybe Katelyn's strong belief in the protection of her Creator hadn't been passed on to her daughter. Whoever really knew why things were the way they were? All Deception knew was how easy it was to get in Celeste's head and take her self worth on a heck of a roller coaster ride.

Deception continued to work his magic, briefly interrupted by Ackmen's entrance. Something was wrong. Ackmen's arrogance no longer surrounded him.

Deception stopped his twirling. "What's wrong with you?"

"Nothing," growled Ackmen. "Get back to work."

Deception did has he was told, only to stop several minutes later. "Ah, Necklim is here isn't he?"

Ackmen cast a look that would have killed him on the spot if he'd had that kind of power. "That's none of your concern. Do your job so the rest of us can get to ours."

Deception muffled his laugh. Seeing a high-ranking demon shudder was a bit amusing for a lesser subordinate such as himself. Before Deception could realize what had happened though, that massive, shuddering demon had him pinned to the wall by his neck.

Ackmen lowered his head and looked Deception in the eye. "Do you find something funny?"

"No, my lord. Not at all." Deception knew better than to squirm or float through Ackmen's hold, which he was perfectly capable of doing. His existence proved more important than a brief reprimand from his leader.

Ackmen let go and pointed to the girl. "Back to work, you insufficient spirit."

Deception ignored his words. He knew his work was necessary, that's the very reason Ackmen was here.

Warmth and peace still radiated around Katelyn, like by some magical force her very bones had sucked these good things into them. It was needed...this peace. She had to remain calm. She'd said this meant war, and she'd meant it. And now, a war was more evident than ever. The fact that Necklim was in her home confirmed it.

Grabbing her Bible off the table she went to the hall and stopped in front of her daughter's door. She knelt down, opened the book, and began praying scriptures out loud.

Necklim was near. She knew, from the past, that his prayers and praise were mixing with hers. Knew that at that very moment they were flooding the gates of Heaven.

Katelyn wasn't sure how long she'd remained there, in the presence of the Lord, guarded by her Warrior, but it didn't feel nearly long enough.

She stood and stretched out her legs. A prayer team was needed. Phone calls were made to her mom, in-laws, her best friend Miranda, as well as to other close friends in the church. And finally to the Pastor. Katelyn knew the power of prayer. She knew prayers, and praise helped increase the power and strength of the Warriors.

"She's made the calls for prayer. I'm going to check in with the Commander to see what our next step will be. I don't know how long we'll be able to wait. There's a threat in the air. One much stronger than what was over Katelyn. I'm calling a meeting."

Nolan nodded and left his post. He followed Necklim to the back yard. Necklim waved his sword, a bright, faint blue light encircled his head, inching its way up through the atmosphere until it found its home in the clouds.

It wasn't long before the other Warriors joined him. "Katelyn has made the calls. The prayer team has been assembled. I'm going to check in with the Commander. Be on your guard. Melti will soon arrive, I'm sure."

Necklim raised his sword, and it met with the tips of his fellow angels, "For the Worthy!"

Ackmen stood by Celeste's window, looking out at the trees that filled the Holcomb's back yard, while he waited impatiently for Deception to finish his orders. Hidden deep within the covering of those trees were the Warriors, he was sure of it. He chipped away at the paint on the window sill and watched for any sudden movements. "They're toying with us," he finally said. He turned towards Deception, "You know they are. Sick beings they are. They enjoy seeing us sweat."

A glowing light in the midst of the trees caused Ackmen to focus his attention back from where it had come. Seconds later the small bright light shot up through the sky. It's brilliance and size alone told of its strength. It meant two things. There were more than three or four Warrior angels, and a prayer team had been formed. "Great. Melti is going to love this. Are you almost done you wretched spirit? We have to get back to Melti."

"A few more minutes," came Deception's response.

The light disappeared. Ackmen waited by the window in hopes of seeing who was with Necklim. Though it didn't matter much. The one Warrior he feared the most had been placed in the Holcomb's home. The coming battle left a weak spot in his in core. Necklim's promise...would it ring true?

CHAPTER FOURTEEN

Steven Steel, the Pastor of Green Hill Christian Church for the past seventeen years, was a middle-aged man, married, with no children of his own. He and Lucinda, his wife of twenty years, lived contently in the small house on the church's property. Pastor Steven enjoyed the luxury of being so close to what he lovingly referred to as his "second home".

Pastor Steven had been at Green Hill Christian, long enough to know when something was amiss in the spiritual life of a member of his small congregation. And something was definitely amiss. The particular situation, and with whom, had up to this point, not been determined. Weeks had passed, leaving the strange feeling that called for aggressive prayer, unclaimed. No prayer requests, no matter how small or large, had eased his troubled spirit.

Not until today.

Today, thanks to a phone call from Katelyn, it had all come together, and finally made sense. Today the unrest inside had mixed and mingled with a little bit hope, and a little bit of understanding.

An attack against Katelyn's daughter was underway.

Once the conversation ended, Pastor Steven did what he knew how to do best.

He prayed.

Not regular, everyday prayers. No. These prayers were mighty for bringing down strongholds and tearing apart wicked schemes of his Creator's enemy. These prayers left demons shaking in their lizard-like skin. His voice wasn't loud, and it didn't need to be, for it was full of authority. An authority that he wasn't afraid to let himself step into, in the name of his Savior.

Spiritual warfare was nothing to mess around with; this the Pastor knew all too well. Since he knew, he had to be ready and aware on all fronts. His prayers not only flooded the gates of Heaven, but they, more often than not, also placed a target on his back.

Lucinda had only seen her husband not make it to the table on a handful of occasions. The man enjoyed his food. Whatever was keeping him, she knew it was of importance. She wondered if it had anything to do with his unrest as of late. If it did, she needed to be in prayer as well. Her husband was a strong man of faith. He didn't back away from anything just because it was difficult. That brought attention to himself at times. She knelt next to the table. The food would wait; she needed to pray.

Ezera, the Warrior flew concealed through the sky. His destination lit up before him like a beacon of light, hope, and power. He landed effortlessly on the roof of Pastor Steven Steel's small home and unfolded the massive wings attached to his body. The feathers danced to the rhythm of the light spring breeze as they lay covering the house in a protective shield. A shield no eye, human or demon could see or penetrate.

Ezera's prayers and praises mixed with the ones breaking through from below. A surge of heated power ran through him, like his very veins were being consumed by a molten liquid, the ever-increasing warmth growing brighter and brighter until it cast a heavenly glow and overtook the shadowy dusk that had fallen on the small Kentucky town.

Pastor Steven finally felt a bit of peace in his spirit. He had no idea how long he'd prayed, but his stomach's rumbling told him it was past dinner time. He vaguely remembered hearing the soft chime ring out, announcing that the food was on the table, but couldn't remember how long ago that had been. This prayer battle had left him peaceful yet drained and hungry. He finished up with an amen, before letting his nose lead him to the wonderful smells from the kitchen. Cold food or not, his body needed some fuel.

"I received a phone call from Katelyn Holcomb," he said as he stepped into the kitchen, unaware that his wife was lost deep in prayer. A smile formed on his lips as he took in the sight of her, head bowed and resting on interlaced fingers. After a few moments, her gaze met his.

"Sorry, dear, didn't realize you were praying."

"No worries." She smiled. "Hand me your plate, and I'll heat it up for you."

Pastor Steve handed the plate in his wife's direction.

"Seems Celeste is going through a hard time right now. Katelyn believes she is under attack. From the few things she told me, I have to say I agree. She has asked for our prayers."

"Oh my. Of course." Lucinda answered as if there wasn't any other option. For her, for them, there wasn't. The dark part of spiritual realm, very much real, weaved and worked throughout the world and the people in it for the destruction of all things good. From the smallest seed of doubt to the biggest, the Enemy showed his power. His power, though, was nothing compared to the Creator's. In that knowledge is where the Steel's strength, peace, and power dwelt.

Ezera landed on the plush carpet in the Steel's living-room. The Guardians over the home joined him. With the first round of prayers complete, he was able to fill the Guardians in on the situation.

"If you notice anything, and I mean anything out of the ordinary, send word to Necklim. We don't know how big this battle will turn out to be, but you can rest assured "small" is far from it."

He met the Guardians' nod with one of his own.

"I'll return soon. Be watchful."

CHAPTER FIFTEEN

Necklim returned to the Holcomb household, twenty more Warriors with him. The days and nights ahead would demand their strength. The Commander said as much.

Necklim landed, drew his sword and twirled it several times in a circular motion above his head. Its light sliced the darkness, signaling for an assembly.

It wasn't long before the other Warriors arrived, not surprised by the number returned with their leader. Each one could feel the evil. It snaked through the air like a venomous snake waiting to sink its teeth into an unexpected victim.

Necklim repeated word for word from the Commander. This battle was going to be bigger than the one nineteen years ago. More significant than the Warriors had fought in quite some time. More Warriors, in fact, were on their way at that very moment. More, still on stand by.

Necklim was just about to give orders when the remaining thirty Warriors joined the gathering.

It didn't take long for the meeting to conclude — each Warrior, stone-faced and ready. Fifty plus glowing white swords met the tip of one another. "For the Worthy!" they shouted.

Warriors dispatched soon after, carried away by wings of white overlapped by a radiant blue. The contrast was breathtaking against the ebony sky. Armor of different colors covered their bodies. All of which housed a sword and shield.

They each went to their post or territory. Guardians in those places were informed. People were covered. Warriors were ready.

Melti and Ackmen, along with a couple of other demons, rode the wind of the night sky, rehearsing plans and attacks. All wrapped up in the joyousness of the occasion, they sought to outdo one another's nasty cackles. When something in the distance caught the bulging red eyes of Melti, his leathery wings, once spread out, now tucked halfway behind his upright body. Could it be? No, it had to be a deception. A decoy. A lie. The light, white, strong, fierce, full, meant more than several Warriors.

"Ackmen!" Oblivious to his master's sudden stop, he turned to face him. "How many Warriors did you say were here?"

"I didn't, Melti. I said by the stream of light there had to be no more than four or five."

"Look!" Melti hissed.

Ackmen turned in the direction of his master's pointy finger. "Oh, no."

"Was the stream of light that bright?"

"No, my lord. Nor was it that big."

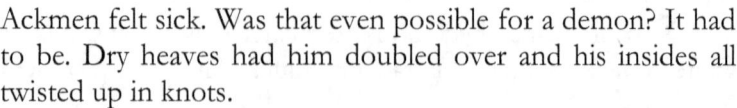

Ackmen felt sick. Was that even possible for a demon? It had to be. Dry heaves had him doubled over and his insides all twisted up in knots.

This was not good. More reinforcements had arrived since this afternoon. A lot more. "Curse you, Necklim."

Ackmen wanted nothing more than for this fight to be over. To what gain was this family, this girl? Surely there was someone else? Some other Burnsten, not covered and guarded by the hosts of Heaven? One they could easily have their way with; one that could as sufficiently turn the tables?

If only.

Asking would only show weakness that he couldn't afford to show. Not now. Not when the grip on Celeste's life was a couple of days away. Melti would do more than torture him, no doubt. He would kill him.

This family was not worth his life. Though he had to wonder if it would be lost soon anyway. Which sword would he rather die from, his master's, or his enemy?

Ackmen's mind was made up. His choice made. "I may go down, but I'll go down fighting," he whispered.

A thump sent him flip-flopping through the air. He regained his composure and slowly drifted back to Melti. "What was that for?" Anger laced his words.

No answer came — only a stare of hate and malice.

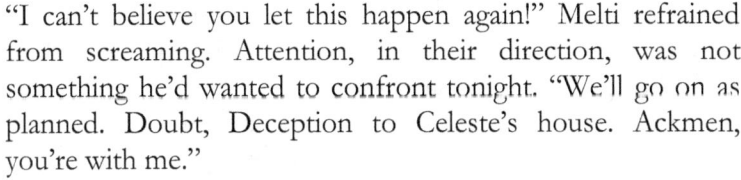

"I can't believe you let this happen again!" Melti refrained from screaming. Attention, in their direction, was not something he'd wanted to confront tonight. "We'll go on as planned. Doubt, Deception to Celeste's house. Ackmen, you're with me."

Melti flew this way and that through the tops of the trees, keeping his focus on the task at hand as much as possible. Though interrupted at times by the nagging reminder of the Warriors strength, their number brought a twinge, brief as it was, to his core. It rested there, not fully letting him enjoy the destruction the next couple nights held.

The enemy always seemed one step ahead. One more person covered, guarded.

Prayers.

They had to be stopped. Who was doing it? Where was it coming from? Melti thought of a new plan, but they'd have to leave Daren's early.

He sank unknowingly through the boy's roof, and slowly drifted down into his room. Daren lay on his stomach, book – their book – in front of him. Ackmen joined Melti; their bony fingers carried their enticing words from their evil minds to Daren's ears. "She's ready. If not, we'll force her. Who waits until they're married anymore? Intimacy is not a treasure. It is a human desire, one that needs to be fulfilled. She will agree, or we'll make her agree."

Several hours passed as these insinuations, ideas, played on repeat, over and over again. Taking root in Daren's heart.

<hr>

A Warrior stood outside Daren's house. The vile filth that Melti filled the young mind with left him sadden and disgusted. He took a step forward, only to be blocked by the powers of the enemy that surrounded the boy's home. Though he couldn't break through them, it didn't stop him from being able to hear the evil intentions the hideous creatures were spewing out. He'd take this information back to Necklim. But for now, he'd stand and pray.

A grotesque face peered down at him from the upstairs window. Meant for intimidation, he was sure, though it failed. It only increased the Warrior's prayer, his praise, his determination. Losing a soul, any soul, to the enemy's side was not on the agenda.

The Warrior unfolded his wings. Their massive size spanned the entire front of the house. His body, prepared, donned in full battle array, was ready for anything tonight. "Ever Ready," he whispered as he peered back into the face of Melti.

CHAPTER SIXTEEN

Not being able to stay stationed in Celeste's room didn't settle well with her Warrior, Nolan. Sure he could go in from time to time, but it wasn't enough. Not to his liking. His whispers, nudges, had to be done quickly and with a grand procession.

Nolan carefully positioned his hand over Celeste. A glowing light, like a controlled lighting bolt, surged and escaped from his large palm. It flickered as it closed the distance between them. A small amount of faith still resided inside his charge. As long as that part was there, no matter how far it had been buried, hope remained. It was a place he could reach. And that he did, with all his might.

The flicker stayed a steady stream, carrying with it peace, love, and truth. All the emotions needed to reach the parts Celeste had hidden away. All the pieces she feared were gone.

They weren't.

The flicker, steady as it was, sent jolts from his form to hers. To the human eyes, it would look like magic. A bolt full of power. Though this power would bring with it no damage, only healing.

Celeste inwardly fought off the acceptance of the truth Nolan poured into her. He wouldn't give up. That wasn't an option. She was his charge, and he took his stance, his oath, her very life, seriously.

His time was coming to an end. The repulsive essence of the enemy had gotten stronger. They were drawing near. Soon he'd have to leave and stand outside her door. His words, nudges, would have to fight their way through the evil that would blanket her. "Celeste," he whispered.

Celeste stopped reading the book on her lap and looked up. Nothing. Though she could have sworn she heard the faintest whisper of her name.

"Hello? Who's there?" she questioned the darkness.

How silly. Or was it. This hadn't been the first time a strange, yet warm, almost protective feeling had come over her.

She turned her attention back to the book and ignored the sensation that she wasn't alone. What she couldn't ignore was the great comfort that began to course through her body, slowly. Peace, love, all the things she wished she had, ignited, like a tiny flame looking for anything to consume so it could grow. It held her still. Frozen. Longing. Waiting. Wondering. Though hidden deep within, hope had remained, clouded by ridiculous lies. By whispers of doubt.

So many things had changed. Time had passed, unrelenting in its pursuit to an end, to claim the weak. Claim the distorted, the wicked. She was one of those now. Maybe not truly wicked, but no doubt weak. She knew. Daren knew. Soon her parents would know it too. Would know what a failure their precious daughter was.

There it was again — that internal struggle. Back and forth, it went. Good, bad. Happy replaced the sad. Light snuffed out by dark. It was real. And it drove her beyond crazy sometimes. The light had its way for now — the goodness. A sliver of joy burst through. A smile. True. Real. That hadn't happened very much over the last few weeks.

It was strange to feel that again. As small as it was. How hard had she become? How distant from her previous self.

She closed the book, determined to enjoy this awareness. Enjoy the faint feeling before it found the bruised, broken, and bitter heart that was now her and fluttered off to some other worthy soul.

In the pits of despair, this was where she lived now. In the agony of her less than brilliant choices. There was only one to blame. She'd take it. Stand boldly for the punishment of her decisions. What else could she do?

A chill pushed out the warmth. Celeste knew it would. It always did.

Doubt and Deception wormed their way through the Warriors and Guardians that were about the Holcomb's home. Being in such company, and not on their territory, weakened them. They sought the refuge that was rightly theirs in the small room down the hall.

They slid through the door, caught off guard by the tall, muscular Warrior. "Flee from here, you disgusting heavenly host!" Deception hissed. A vile stench seeped from him towards Nolan.

A sword, lit up with power, put an end to any further advances from the demons. Deception and Doubt scrambled to either side of the room, leaving plenty of space for Nolan to pass by. A fight against him would only end their demise.

Doubt turned to Deception, "What was he doing in here?"

"What he's been doing since the enemy got here, trying to place a ray of hope in our dear Celeste. It's nothing to worry about. His time with her is short-lived; it won't do any good."

"Are you certain?"

Deception didn't answer. Instead, he focused on completing his mission tonight. Getting Celeste to Daren was the only thing that mattered.

Ideas wove through the air like missiles locked on a target. The first one hit its MARK. The demons, the nasty creatures they are, smiled with glee as Celeste took the bait. She'd set the book on the nightstand and picked up the phone. The text had been sent. All was in motion.

Doubt had remained unmoved up until this point. A lizard-like appendage edged into the side of Celeste's face. Searing imaginations entered her already spinning head and fragile heart.

"Daren doesn't love you," it hissed. "There's only one thing he wants from you."

Next came Deception with twisted lies of his own. "If you give him what he wants, everything will be fine. He will love you."

A small light from the device clutched in her hand lit up the space directly in front of her. Highlighting the confused expression on her face, though neither creature needed it to see the distortions.

◆ ◆ ◆ ◆ ◆

"Do you like me?" Celeste had asked. Daren had responded with a yes. The answer to her next question wasn't as concrete, or as fast. "I love you. Do you love me?"

She'd done it. Put her heart out there on the line. What

did she have to lose? Was she sure this was love? There had been nothing to compare it to.

An overly expected vibration caused her to jump. His response. Finally. Funny how minutes had a way of feeling like hours when you nervously waited for an answer. "Prove it," he'd said.

Could she? So close before, but now? Why couldn't those three words be enough? They would've been for her.

In return, she had made him wait for a response. One she wasn't sure she wanted to give. She hadn't remembered typing the word on her screen that stared back at her. But there it was. Four letters. In black, followed by a question mark.

When?

CHAPTER SEVENTEEN

A wrong choice made. One covered deep in the grips of deception. Nolan could feel it hanging in the air. It taunted him. Anger, righteous, developed within him. It would draw his fellow Warrior, his leader, to his side. It always did.

As if on cue, Necklim appeared. Apprehension on his face. Nolan was aware that his leader knew the righteous anger could only mean one thing.

"What's happened?" Necklim asked.

"Her decision was made. It will happen tonight."

"Already?" Necklim asked.

Nolan's celestial body shook. Ready to fight.

"In time, my friend. In time. Now is not it."

Necklim's encouragement had always brought Nolan's emotions down a notch. In check. Sure, he knew his leader was right. Nothing would, could, happen until the right time. He knew that. Though he desired not to, this was always the hardest time for Nolan. Standing along the sidelines, like a player waiting to be called into the game.

"Should I stay here?" Deep down, Nolan already knew the answer. He asked, anyway.

"Yes. Inform me when Celeste leaves. I will send others with you when she does," Necklim responded.

Nolan fought the twinge Necklim's words doused over

him and instead asked, "Do you know who?"

"Not yet. The Commander will tell me before the time arrives."

"So be it." His answer was short. To the point. Maybe a little on edge. Necklim patted his back before disappearing, leaving him staring at Celeste's door alone, waiting for her to move. Waiting to follow. Waiting for battle.

Katelyn placed her Bible on the bed. The atmosphere around her changed. Necklim was near.

"Katelyn." His whisper sent chills down her spine. The tone – that tone – meant something big was about to happen. Fear and Doubt tried to sink in their claws, but she cast them away. There was no time for that. The soul of her daughter was in a dangerous position. One she remembered being in herself.

Katelyn rose from her chair, shoulders back, concentration etched the lines of her face.

"Necklim?"

A bright light filled the space beside her. An outline of wings came into view first, followed by the ivory white skin and blonde hair she had become used to all those years ago.

"You need to pray." He said. "Hard. All night, for Celeste."

Torn between asking details and not wanting to know she settled on asking a question she already knew the answer to. One that latched onto the hope inside her. "Will a Warrior be with her?"

"Yes. Nolan is her Warrior. He will be with her. He will do what he is able. As you already know there's a certain distance, he must remain, until she calls upon the Lord."

She nodded. "Yes. I know." The Warrior started to fade. Leaving behind the dimly lit space, he'd filled so brightly.

Katelyn called for Trevor. The look on his wife's face was all that was needed. His arms embraced her as together they fell on their knees.

Tears streamed down her cheeks as a low cry bubbled up from within. Sobs turned into prayers. Ones full of power, authority, boldness. What this night held for her only child, she did not know. But her confidence was in the One who did. Fear would not overtake her tonight, for fear was a weapon of the enemy. And she was a child of the Creator, Commander, the King.

His weapons of power, love, and a sound mind were hers. A belief that all things work together for the good of those that love Him was her foundation. The fact her enemy had done been defeated was her shield. And her praise. Her praise was her sword. All she intended on using.

Though Necklim could no longer be seen, Katelyn was aware of him. He was close. So close, she felt the soft touch of his wings against her arms. Her angel. Her Warrior, sent again to stand in the cap for her. How blessed she had been then. How blessed she was now.

* * *

Nolan found Necklim standing over Trevor and Katelyn. The glow that radiated from him proved his power. Demonstrated the belief of those he guarded – those he would soon go into battle for.

"Necklim. Celeste's gone."

"I know," Necklim responded. "Reneese and Nalof are to go with you. Make haste. Whisper into the wind if you must, but never stop trying to reach her."

"As you say, it will be done."

Renesse and Nalof manifested next to Nolan. Their swords raised, tips together, they shouted, "For the Worthy!"

Nolan slightly folded his massive wings behind him and darted upwards. Followed by his fellow Warriors, their heavenly bodies vanished through the boards, drywall, and beams that made up the ceiling above them. A chill, not caused by weather, brought the three heavenly bodies to a sudden stop. They remained motionless, scanning the world below them.

"There." Nolan pointed. In the cover of the trees was a body, hunched over, its eyes closed. With precise precision, Nolan maneuvered through the trees and landed as close as possible, careful not yet to alert the demons guarding the young girl.

Reneese and Nalof stood on either side of Nolan. "Keep alert and on guard," he warned.

Nolan raised his hands in Celeste's direction. Slender streams of golds and yellows flowed towards her, penetrating the evil veil that held her captive in its dark prison.

"Celeste." He coated his voice with the compassion only heavenly beings held. "You don't have to fear us. We won't you. We are here to help. I am here to help."

Nothing.

He would not be deterred. "My name is Nolan. I'm here in front of you. I'm not a figment of your imagination."

Her fear was great. It crashed against him with such force that it took him by surprise. She looked up, her body ridged, though he could hear her heart hammering against her chest.

"Celeste. Why are you running? Why are you trying to fill the void that's grown in your heart by giving yourself to someone undeserving of it?

"H...How do you know this?"

"I am your Warrior. I was sent to fight for you, Celeste."

"Fight for me?"

The doubt she felt rang strong in her words. "Why would you want to fight for me?"

A shadowy figure appeared behind Celeste. Deception. One of her oppressors.

"You are being deceived, child. The enemy wants you. He too is fighting for you."

Small hands covered her ears. A scream, shrill, full of released pain traveled through the branches and leaves around her.

Nolan stood unmoved, observing Deception, waiting for his next attack on the girl.

Celeste rose, moments later. An empty look filled her eyes. Her moves, mechanical almost, led her deeper into the darkness. Deeper into the lie being weaved around her. Through her.

"You don't have –."

A red sword covered in flames appeared before Nolan's face, cutting off his words. Green eyes once close to the ground were now at his level.

"Back off, Warrior," Deception hissed.

The warning meant nothing to Nolan. He would not stand down until there was no other choice. He grabbed hold of the sword, fought through the heat it put off and flung it backward, sending Deception with it.

"You don't scare me, spirit. Nor do I take orders from you. I will not back off."

CHAPTER EIGHTEEN

Celeste's quick response hadn't been on Melti's radar. Nothing about this mission had stuck to his meticulous planning, why should tonight be any different? Leaving Daren's was no longer an option. Though finding out who was praying was a must. It had to be dealt with, and soon.

The enemy was a force to be reckoned with on their own. When they had the prayers of believers behind them, they were just about unbeatable. Just about. That sliver gave Melti hope. It had to. He held onto that hope with all his strength.

The trees rustled in the distance. The girl was close. Melti called for Doubt.

"Go get the others. Send some out to find the prayer warriors. Dismantle them, by any means necessary."

"She's almost at the door," Ackmen said, pulling Melti's attention from the departing figure.

"Any sign of her Warrior?"

"No."

"Playing hide and seek, how nice."

The ding-dong of the doorbell rang throughout the house just as Deception showed up. "Master, I have news. I'm afraid you're not going to like it."

Melti's rage rumbled in the back of his throat. "What is it?" he growled between clenched teeth.

"The girl, she doesn't have just one Warrior. She has three."

Melti's large charcoal-colored chest rose and fell with intensity. Three Warriors over one person? Not good. It couldn't be.

"Who's the main one?"

"Nolan, my lord."

Melti laughed. Wisps of putrid yellow vapor covered the three creatures. "Nolan." He turned towards Ackmen. "And you were worried about Necklim."

"Don't be so sure he won't show up." Ackmen bristled.

"Oh, I'm counting on it. Once his fellow Warriors' are no longer with us, I'm sure he'll be the first one here."

<hr />

Daren opened the door. The thrill of claiming his prize plastered on his face. "Hey." He stepped to the side, then closed the door behind them. "So you're going to go through with it this time, huh?"

"That's the plan," Celeste whispered.

"Plan?" Daren raised his brow. "No, no plan. You will. Why else would you be here?"

"I suppose you're right."

"Let's go then," Daren said as he wrapped his fingers around her arm, yanking her behind him.

"Daren, wait, please."

"What?" His voice was cold.

"Can't we talk for a bit first?"

"Why? So you can change your mind? No, I don't think so."

He pulled on her arm again. Her restraint only fueled his desire. He'd had enough of her uncertainty, enough of her games. Showing up was her own mistake. Her own downfall. He'd been patient long enough. He'd waited long enough. It was time.

He turned and twisted her arm. The flinch, the fear, in the scared expression looking back at him, swayed not his intention. He would have what he wanted, and he wanted her.

"Daren, please...you're hurting me."

He stopped. "And you don't think you've hurt me," he screamed. Turning he brought his other arm in the air, slung it forward and struck her cheek. Brown hair flew out as her head jerked to the side. A trickle of blood sat on her lip.

"Daren, what are you doing?" she cried, through uncontrolled sobs.

Another slap stung her face.

He jerked her to him and whispered in her ear, "What does it look like I'm doing?"

He left no time for her to respond. He curled his fingers then sent them forward. His hard knuckles met her soft skin. Her knees buckled. Her eyes closed. He laughed.

◆ ◆ ◆ ◆

Daren, nothing more than a mere puppet, his willingness to let hate breed inside himself, made him easy to control. To manipulate. Melti and Ackmen stood behind the boy, entranced in an inner pleasure no rational being could comprehend. "I chose well," Melti said.

On and on the two massive creatures filled Daren's head with impure thoughts. Ideas. They fueled his impatience. His overwhelming desire for control. Until all that mattered was getting what he wanted. Despite anyone else. Their feelings, her feelings, were no longer a concern — just his.

Melti stopped his control of the boy for a moment. Thin dark skin covered his eyes, and a grin split his dark, rough lips. Evil, in great numbers, drew near. Their anticipation for bloodshed surged through the night air, igniting a massive frenzy among them. He loved it. The power. The chaos. The thrill of it all. It made him feel alive. He let the possibilities to come sink in. The casualties of his enemies would leave them weak. Unguarded.

Soon, he'd sink the pointed claws of his long dark fingers into the heart of Katelyn's precious daughter. The anticipation of Celeste's devotion to him sent an unbridled excitement through him. One he hadn't felt in quite some time. Winning over Katelyn's daughter was big. One that showed power, authority, strength, cleverness. Slander. Deceit. This very moment had been talked about since the day of her birth. It was a long time coming, and now it was finally here.

The enemy may have taken Latar out nineteen years ago, but Latar he was not. Melti planned to make sure everyone – angel, human, and demon alike – knew who he was. Remembered his name.

A sudden disturbance ceased his demented enjoyment. His eyes, hidden no more, blazed with the yellow intensity of a raging inferno. Bright, hot, and full of fire – as a look of destruction – overtook them. He turned towards the window to his right where the brief flicker of blue light had caught his attention. They were not alone.

A growl reverberated through Melti's jagged teeth as he glared into the midnight blue eyes of the Warrior watching him. He'd expected the meddling, pesky, enemy of light to show up sometime.

"Welcome to the fun, Nolan. Are you enjoying the show?" Pure evil pulled up the side of Melti's lip. "Here we go, boys!" he shouted.

Melti leaped through the window, leaving it intact, as charcoal leather transitioned through it. He pulled his sword from its sheath and sliced at the Warrior in front of him. Nolan had been ready for Melti's attack. He grabbed the curved end of the demon's scimitar in both hands and snapped it in two as Melti flew past him.

Melti took only a moment to recuperate. Again he came at Nolan, arms out in front of him, nails like razors ready to slice through the heavenly being, sending him back to his realm of safety, and security.

Again Nolan was on guard. Melti felt the burn of holiness creep up his arm as Nolan grabbed onto him with all his strength. Their bodies tumbled through the dark sky in a death roll as Melti tried unsuccessfully to break free from the Warrior's hold.

His arm burned. He covered the scream that begged to be let lose with a deep growl. The leader of the army of Hell could not show weakness. The shriek that begged to fill the air was trapped deep in the throat of the demon. Nolan flung him back and forth until finally letting go, sending him off into the night. This small battle was over. But the war had just begun.

CHAPTER NINETEEN

Celeste moaned as she came to, blinking her eyes several times before opening them completely. Dampness and darkness surrounded her. *Where am I? What happened?* She couldn't remember. Didn't know if she ever wanted to.

A rancid smell sent her stomach into full objection. She forced the urge back down her throat and focused on pushing her limp body up off the cold concrete floor. Pain came with each push. It ran through her — every muscle. Every joint screamed out in a rebellious protest. Her vision adjusted to the darkness.

What looked like shelves lined the back wall. It was what sat on those shelves that she couldn't see. Feel, though, that was another story.

"Hello?" she called. Her voice was full of uncertainty.

A low voice in the darkness responded. It called to her. She felt it. Heard it. It appealed to her very soul. It longed to become one with it, with her. It offered solitude, healing peace. Though the feeling of it, like an awful aftertaste, left something to be desired. It brought with it no comfort. No sense of hope or love. Just hatred.

Celeste ignored it. Tried to focus on what happened, why she was where she was.

Images, fuzzy, popped in and out of her confused

thoughts. She gasped. *No. No, that couldn't have happened. Daren would never do that. Would he?* Did she know him well enough? No, she didn't.

Screams, followed by horrible cries of pain, came back to her. She felt her lip. Busted, once bloody, from the feel of the sticky substance. Fresh tears escaped her eyes as the last thing she remembered happening entered her thoughts. It would remain etched on her young heart forever.

Daren pulling apart her shirt played on repeat. Like a movie stuck on a scene that had been watched way too many times she became stuck in that one moment, in that one spot. *How could he? Why did he? Where is he?* All were questions left without any answers.

The demons around her laughed. Delighted in her pain. They fed off it. Grew strength off her fear and sorrow. Melti was among them. "What now, dear girl?" he asked. Though Celeste hadn't heard Melti's question, she answered all the same.

"I know I should've asked you sooner," Celeste said. All the evilness around her held their putrid misty breathe and set on edge as they listened. Waiting for her surrender.

It didn't come.

"Help me, Lord."

"NO!!!" Melti screamed.

Celeste flinched at the growl of displeasure that filled her ears, and pulled her knees close, hugging them as tightly as she could.

A warmth. The same warmth she'd felt before enveloped her. Bits at a time the darkness was driven away until no space was not engulfed by glorious light. Shrieks, curses, and screams could be heard, but she was unable to see from where they came. The three glowing beings standing around her blocked everything else. A wall stood between her and whatever was on the other side. For that, she was thankful.

"Celeste, we must go."

She looked up. Eyes as deep and dark as the abyss somehow extended comfort as they bore into her. "Nolan?"

"Yes. You are safe now. But we must get you out of here."

Shock held relief at bay, but her body responded anyway. "Where am I?"

"You are in the basement of Daren's house. He is upstairs, asleep. Follow me."

One step at a time they climbed the long wooden staircase. It wobbled beneath her weight, just as her knees did. At last, the door that had hidden her crushed body away from the world opened. Freedom was only a few steps away.

Or was it?

The possibility of this night holding her trapped inside herself forever was real. It would never be forgotten.

Nolan opened the front door. Celeste stepped out. An angel on either side and one behind. But she could go no farther. Her eyes widened. Hideous creatures of all sizes and shapes hissed and lunged in her direction.

"They won't get to you as long as we're here. Keep focused on the Creator and pray. Everything will be fine."

Celeste gulped.

"Pray, Celeste." Nolan encouraged. But could she pray to a Creator that turned His back to her attack?

Doubt felt a tug, though small, it was enough. He slithered towards Celeste, only to be pushed back by the electric pulses from Reneese's sword. "You are to come no further."

Celeste tried to hear what Nolan whispered to the angel behind them, but her mind just wasn't able to comprehend what was going on before her. These things, these horrid beings. These demons. They did exist. The fight was real. Good and evil were before her. No longer could either side be ignored. No longer could she put these creatures in a fairy-tale, make-believe world. No longer.

Her mom had been right. Her young self was not ready for this.

Necklim stood guard over Katelyn and Trevor a couple of hours before receiving word of Celeste's call for help. Nalof informed him of the masses of demons that surround Mack and Daren's home.

Finding out Nolan had already had a confrontation with Melti was a bit of a surprise. It seemed not only the small demons and spirits were on edge, but all of them were. Melti had held his cool much better nineteen years ago. The lead demon having a slip up hadn't crossed Necklim's mind. Melti's hunger for vengeance might be his final downfall.

Nalof left to return to Nolan and Reneese, leaving Necklim and Malkia to guide Katelyn and Trevor to their daughter.

"We need to get Katelyn and Trevor to Daren's as soon as possible. Celeste is outside and waiting."

Necklim's sudden brightness filled the room. "Katelyn, we must go. Celeste needs you."

There were no questions asked, only hurried obedience. She grabbed Trevor's arm, "We have to go." They raced out the door. Katelyn slipped behind the wheel of the car and followed the glowing light that was her Warrior.

Necklim didn't know if Celeste would be able to see everything her mom was taking in when they pulled up. Though she probably would feel it. He'd been told she had a sense for that kind of thing now. He could believe that.

More than just the disappearance of the sun blotted out

the moon's soft glow. Eyes – yellow, green, and red in color – followed not only Necklim's every move but the car behind him as well. Knowing who sat within the moving structure, no doubt had them all a little high strung, uneasy.

Most were there that night, long ago. Seeing Latar, their leader, destroyed, wouldn't have been easily swept from their memories. Neither, though, would the victory of the prize in front of them.

Necklim's wings flapped gently as he lowered at the end of Daren's drive. Katelyn rolled to a stop next to him. "This is as far as I can go," he said. "Pull up to the front of the house. Celeste is there with Nolan."

If Katelyn could see what surrounded them, she didn't say. Not that she would. She didn't cower easily. Necklim knew that. She'd come far in her journey. In her life. In her belief. She knew to whom she belonged, and she wasn't afraid of what her Lord had already beaten.

As he watched the scene unfold before him, he was taken back in time. A car. A girl. A two-story house. The sky full of demons, even more so full of heavenly Warriors yet to be seen. All so familiar. All so surreal.

Katelyn let the car roll to a stop. The door swung open, and she jumped out and hurried in her daughter's direction. Necklim kept alert and his hand on the handle of his sword. Things were going too smoothly. What are you up to, Melti?

He didn't like the calmness. He nodded to his fellow Warriors. "Ever ready," he warned.

CHAPTER TWENTY

There amid three Warriors stood her daughter, shoulders slightly hunched over. Her shirt, torn, hung in a disheveled fashion. Beautiful black hair that had been neatly held high off her neck a few hours ago rested loosely next to her ear. Green eyes, so full of life and innocence, now darted back and forth with an undesirable knowledge.

Katelyn grabbed Celeste and pulled her in close. "It's okay. I'm here. I've got you. I love you."

Never in Katelyn's life had she remembered a time when her heart had been full of so much hurt, pain. Uncontrollable sobs had her body trembling. For a moment, she let herself grieve what was taken away from her daughter. For a moment, she let her love flow through streams over her cheeks and onto her daughter's head.

And then Katelyn straightened herself and looked at Celeste. "Are you okay?" A dumb question but she had to ask. "We need to get you to the hospital."

Katelyn turned to Trevor, his tilted head and narrow-eyes confirmed he again wasn't able to see what she could. Maybe that was for the best? "Trevor, we need to get her to the hospital."

"I'm not going anywhere just yet, Mom. I know you can see what's out there, just like I can. You need to fight. You need to pray."

Katelyn looked at her daughter. "And you need to be seen by a doctor."

"I will, Mom. After you take care of business." Her daughter's smile eased a little bit of the brokenness.

She watched as Nolan folded Celeste under his protective wing. "Reneese and I will watch over her, and I'll send Nalof with you. Go"

"I'll stay with her as well," Trevor said, knowing Katelyn struggled with doing what needed to be done. "No, Dad. I'm fine. These tough guys will keep me safe. Go with, Mom."

Katelyn nodded her agreement. If Celeste wanted, needed some time, they'd give it. Knowing Warriors were with her made that decision a little easier. "Come on, Trevor."

A silent prayer for her daughter's heart floated up towards heaven as she turned and walked a few steps away.

Eyes, so many, filled with such malice, bore into her.

To bad for them, that didn't bother her anymore.

Arms stretched towards heaven, her silent praise and prayers turned into whispers that ended in a bold authority. Messing with her was one thing. Messing with her child was another.

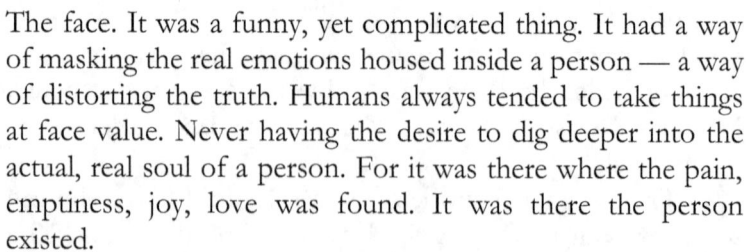

The face. It was a funny, yet complicated thing. It had a way of masking the real emotions housed inside a person — a way of distorting the truth. Humans always tended to take things at face value. Never having the desire to dig deeper into the actual, real soul of a person. For it was there where the pain, emptiness, joy, love was found. It was there the person existed.

Nolan looked past the mask Celeste's face held. Past the brave girl, she was trying to be, deep into her soul. Pain was alive and well, swelling, gaining more momentum like a raging sea fighting against the forceful winds. His heart, though heavenly, ached at what he saw inside.

"Celeste?"

The girl didn't move. Didn't take her eyes from the woman standing a little way in front of them. "I'll never be like her."

Nolan's stare froze Deception in his tracks. He would not allow them to get anywhere near his charge again. "That's good."

He looked out at Katelyn. A fire had been ignited and was burning brightly, mesmerizing like the flicker of flames.

"What do you mean, good?" His statement had puzzled his charge.

"You were not meant to be like her. You my dear, Celeste are not your mom. She is not you."

"She's so confident."

"She wasn't always so sure of herself, Celeste. You shouldn't judge when you don't know the whole story."

"Not sure I want to."

"You're living out your own."

"Yeah."

A towering dark figure landed with such heaviness the ground in front of them shook. Nolan positioned the girl behind him. His wings spread out, separating the creature from his target. "Melti."

"Nolan. Must you prolong the inevitable? Hand her over, and we'll be on our way."

"Never going to happen."

Celeste's hope was draining, like a plug that had held it in place had been pulled, freeing it to twist and twirl into oblivion.

Nolan didn't bother with hushed tones anymore. The time for that had passed. He spoke, concern in his voice. Urgency pushing the words from his mouth through the air in front of him and into the ears of his charge.

Melti pulled his sword from its sheath, with slow movements. The look of pure hell on his contoured face. "Ready to play, Heavenly Warrior?"

Nolan stepped forward. Reneese took his place guarding Celeste.

"No, Melti. But I am ready to fight."

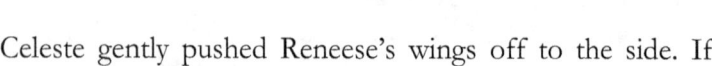

Celeste gently pushed Reneese's wings off to the side. If a fight was going to happen because of her, she wanted to witness it at least.

Melti stepped forward, Nolan's tan skin moved with the tense muscles underneath it. His shoulders rotated in tiny circular motions several times before the sword in his hand pointed towards the sky above. "For the Worthy!" he shouted, then lunged towards the creature in front of him. Swords struck each either mid-air. Clashing like metal workers hammering their vision into submission, fitting each imperfect piece against the next until it comes out as one of perfection.

Perfection. That's what Nolan was to her. Powerful. Beautiful. Wise. Loving. All the things she felt she wasn't worthy of. How could such a perfect being go into battle for one so imperfect? All the times she pushed away his words of encouragement. All the times she closed off her heart to receive his guidance. Why had the Lord wanted to fight for her at all?

Immersed in her thoughts, the fight blurred in the close

distance. It had to be love. What else could it be? One so willing to fight for one so undeserving. Her memory took her back to what she had last read in the Bible. A man. Beaten, bruised, laughed at, mocked, had been placed on a wooden cross, left there to die. He was innocent but found guilty. He had the power to remove Himself from that burden, from the curse – though He did no such thing. For there, He died. Why? What held Him there? She could find no other answer, but the one she started with.

Love.

Swords swayed hitting the armor of the one on its opposite end. Celeste watched in disbelief as Melti overtook Nolan. Pushing his towering body over with his own. Nolan lay on the ground, Melti's sword to his throat. His words were taunting the Warrior beneath him.

Celeste's breath couldn't find its way out of her lungs, like it was stuck in a maze, lost, not knowing which way to turn.

"Help him!" She screamed, but Reneese didn't move. "I'm sorry I can't leave you. My orders are to stay with you."

"Orders?" Did she hear his words correctly? She couldn't have.

Her hands shook. Her mind raced. *I have to help him somehow. I have to do something!* Against her better judgment, she placed one foot in front of the other, only to be stopped after three steps. "What are you doing? Let me go! If you won't help him, then I will!"

Melti's voice, sinister, followed her declaration. "Isn't that sweet. She thinks she can save you, Nolan." Melti's horrid laugh was like a smack in the face.

"Pray, Celeste." She could hardly hear Nolan, through the noise, through her fears.

"I don't know if I can."

"You can. You must."

Nolan's words had become more faint with each one spoken.

She looked up at Reneese, his once gray eyes now a golden glow. It wasn't that he didn't want to help his fellow Warrior. It was that he couldn't. She could see that now. Orders had to be obeyed. It's what kept things in order.

"Will my prayers really help him?"

"They will."

CHAPTER TWENTY-ONE

Late. It was too late. Celeste's eyes widened, her heart hammered, a cry filled the air but did nothing to stop the glowing red sword held by the leathery, clawed hand from plunging through the chest of the Warrior beneath it. Her Warrior.

The world around her grew silent as each angel and demon looked upon the injured Angel, sword still sticking up, held in place by the muscles it had sliced through.

Celeste ran to Nolan. Not caring about the evil that still stood over him. The wetness from the dew on the grass soaked through her jeans as she fell at Nolan's side. Muddy stains would now forever be woven into the faded blue fabric. Such is how she felt — a soiled soul. One stained with the awful truth of a world she didn't know existed. A world with such evil, yet a world with much love. How could that be?

"Nolan." She ran her hand across his forehead and down his cheek.

His eyes fluttered, "Pray, Celeste."

A battle waged within. Would the Lord hear her prayers? "Will they be heard, Nolan?"

"You know what you have to do."

And she did. But she struggled all the same. Pride was a

powerful tool of the enemy. She placed her hand on the armor that covered almost all of Nolan's chest. Almost. "I don't know if I can forgive Daren. The Lord isn't fond of unforgiveness."

How Nolan could smile at a time like this was beyond her reasoning. "No," he said. "I imagine you can't." Nolan sucked in a breath before he continued. The prayers of others were felt, but it was a slow process. So much evil, so many small battles being fought, so much coverage needed over and around this one place had his healing process on slow. Celeste's prayers would help. He had to keep talking.

"But the Lord can. He will help you."

"Oh yes, I'm sure the Lord will help a guilt-ridden girl like her. One full of shame and well, you heard it your self, unforgiveness." Melti laughed. "I'll leave you two to say your goodbyes, but I'll be back for you. You will be mine before the night is through." A hiss like a snake coiled around her, tightening until breath could not escape. She watched him move away. No doubt going after her mother. She looked back to Nolan. His eyes were closed.

"How does the Lord know anything about forgiveness?" she muttered. The question absentmindedly flowed through her lips before she even thought about it. The answer was already known. "He forgives us."

Nolan nodded his head in agreement. "Yes. He does."

Celeste bowed her head, pushing back all the thoughts and feelings that vied for her attention. Only one thing mattered right now — her soul – and where it stood with its Creator.

"Father, forgive me," Celeste whispered. Tears streamed down her face as she continued to pray. Until finally, tense muscles started to relax. She didn't realize how much she'd missed talking with the Lord. Her Lord. Her Creator. The One that gave her strength. The One that filled her with unspeakable peace. It felt good. The shame, hurt, pain, the guilt were all being washed away.

Praise flowed. Demons cried out at the unseen weapon hitting them with such powerful blows. Nolan had wrapped his hand around hers, grip renewed. He was growing stronger. She felt it. His dark eyes now glowed with the same golden hue as Reneese's.

He was back. Her Warrior was back.

"How do you feel, Celeste?"

"Better. Like a freshly washed garment. Dirt and grime no longer a part of it."

"Forgiven?"

Celeste nodded her head. "Forgiven."

———— ◆ ◆ ◆ ◆ ————

Melti landed in front of Katelyn. The blonde-haired, white-winged Warrior behind her might be enough to scare off a lesser demon. Not him. He was not Ackmen. He would not run and hide.

No, instead he would conquer this woman. Winning one Burnsten would accomplish much, but it simply wasn't enough for Melti. He wanted Katelyn as well. He wanted to end the prayers, the praise that was continually offered towards Heaven, and focus it on him. He'd allow the trouble she'd caused to be erased from his memory, once she and her beloved daughter bowed down to him.

A tingle coursed through his muscles, they bulged under his skin. His senses had awakened more than they ever had. Tonight would be a good night. Tonight the enemy would fall. Tonight would be his.

He pulled the one sword he had left and pointed it out in front of him, and pushed through the pain of the heavenly barrier. He charged straight ahead, driven by pure hate through the pain, and the forming blisters. He would have her, or he would die trying.

He flew overhead towards the enemy behind her. The one protecting her. He brought down his sword, but it didn't strike its target. He swung again, and again, but the sword of his enemy stopped it. He backed off, taking the fight to the sky. In the middle of all the other defeats and victories that it held, here he could move. Here he had speed. Here he had victory.

He spun in a circular motion, gaining speed as he traveled past fellow demons and angels, Necklim still far behind. He changed his direction, and like a fired bullet, cut through the sky at top speed, ready to take down whatever had the nerve to get in his way.

His sword out in front of him, he aimed with straight precision at one of the only unprotected places on the enemy. His side.

Necklim had turned and stopped just where Melti hoped he would. A sword, red with flames slipped through the hole on the side of his armor. Puncturing Necklim's side and exiting out the other.

Still, that didn't satisfy the uncontrollable desire they had been birthed inside the demon. He flew, just as fast and powerful as he had been until at last the ground rose up to meet them, and Necklim's body smashed against it.

CHAPTER TWENTY-TWO

Time drug by in slow motion. Sounds faded. Appearances blurred. His breath came in forced labors. Hands, as strong as they were, weakened around the blade protruding from his side. He fell, all twelve feet of him, unto the ground.

"Necklim! No!"

Katelyn ran to her fallen Warrior, fell to her knees and with shaky fingers moved aside the blonde hair that covered the rugged ivory face. Her eyes watered only for a moment. Angels didn't die.

Anger replaced the sorrow. She stood, head raised, shoulders back, and looked into the eyes of Necklim's attacker. No trace of fear. No trace doubt. Only boldness.

Melti towered above her. An evil grin on his thin, leathery lips.

"I wouldn't be so quick to rejoice, Melti. You have not won. You will never win."

Melti stepped back. Each spoken word laced with truth and courage pierced his charcoal skin and sunk in deep like that of an arrow in its prey. Any thought, no matter how remotely small, of regaining Katelyn slipped from his mind. It would never happen. He knew that now, though it was too late.

Pride had gotten the better of him. Pride always did.

Twinges followed the hushed groans he couldn't repress. Every word caused damage. Weakness.

He tried to respond. Tried to come back against her verbal assault, but there was no pause. Katelyn continued to come forward focused on nothing else but him.

A glance towards where her Warrior fell informed him not only of Necklim's disappearance but of the daughter and her Warriors as well.

A blue light appeared to his right. Another on his left, and right next to the troublesome woman in front him, appeared her daughter. The same determined look rested on her similar features. The young girl opened her mouth. Bright light, tinted with blue, carried her words of truth straight to him. The impact more painful than her mother's, had left two-inch deep burns in their wake.

No longer able to hold back the shrieks, he let them escape through his jagged teeth. His fellow demons fell still and silent. Filled with confusion, they looked upon their leader. Taking down Necklim had stirred their ranks, had given them a false sense of hope, of victory. The sight before them took that all away.

"Attack them!" Melti yelled through his increasing screams.

No demon came to his rescue. Surround by heavenly Warriors and blocked off in front by the girl that had caused him such pain and her mother – he was left to fight alone.

Hoping to slip through their encampment, Melti turned, back towards the woman and the girl. His eyes widened. Hadn't he taken this one down? "Nolan?"

"Ever ready, Melti. Ever ready."

Melti watched as the Warrior lifted his sword. The glowing, flickering blues and whites around it held his demise within them. He knew it. His time was over. His reign finished. With a final shrill of the demon, the heavenly blade sliced through him. Where a proud, massive demon once stood, only a pile of burnt ash remained.

Nolan looked around, ready to confront any others. There was no need. Thin wings carried hideous mangled bodies in the opposite direction. Silhouetted against the fading light of the moon.

Celeste didn't want to watch. Even though the fleeing demons meant victory, she'd seen enough. Heard enough. Instead, she focused her gaze on Nolan. The sides of his black hair were caught up in the wind flowing through the breeze. She smiled. Her Warrior. He'd been through a lot on her behalf. Though he would say, it was an honor, his calling – what he was created to do. That was him.

Her mom's arm wrapped around her shoulder. "You okay?" she heard her ask.

"Yeah. I think I am."

Silence sat between the Holcomb family and the remaining angels, though it didn't last long. "Mom, what about Necklim? Will he be okay?"

"I've never seen a Warrior hurt that bad before." They all looked towards Nolan, hoping for a definite answer.

"It will take him a while to heal, but he will be okay." Nolan smiled. "We can be hurt, but we are immortal. There's no end for us unless it is by the Creator Himself."

Relief was heard in the sighs of the mother and daughter next to him. He couldn't help but let out one of his own.

"We will escort you to the hospital. There your Guardians will take over once again."

"Is this over now?" Celeste asked. Though she tried hard to hide the hope in her voice, it hadn't worked.

"For now," Nolan replied.

"Great," Celeste sighed.

"You know, I think that's a famous line for these Warriors. If I recall correctly, I was told the same thing." Katelyn chuckled. A little more light-hearted since the battle was over.

"Maybe so." Nolan's grin was contagious. It spread over the face of his charge. "I will be back, should you ever need me again."

"You better." Celeste held her arm up, fingers drawn into a fist and waited. Nolan laughed. She laughed. "Don't leave me hanging, Nolan."

He tapped her small fist with one two sizes more prominent. "I would never."

Trevor, Katelyn, and Celeste pulled up to the hospital just before sunrise. Their faces, bodies full of nothing but exhaustion. Nolan dismissed the Warriors that accompanied him and Reneese, and then followed the small family through the revolving glass door.

Nolan filled in the Guardians, before saying his goodbyes to the girls that had found their way to the couch. Warriors in their own right. He had to admit. Both strong, spiritually. Both tenacious when they wanted to be. Even with all Celeste had been through, she was able to receive and extend what would help set her free.

Forgiveness.

There was no way Nolan couldn't respect that. Some

humans had a hard time forgiving. He couldn't understand why.

"What should we do now?" Celeste questioned.

Nolan's slightly curled lips answered, "Rest."

DISCUSSION QUESTIONS

1. Have you ever wondered if the battle for your soul is real?

2. Have there ever been times in your life where you've done something and can't quite figure out why?

3. Have you ever had trouble with forgiveness, be it forgiving yourself or someone else?

4. Have you ever felt unforgivable?

Can I tell you something?
God forgives! Jesus forgives!
God loves YOU so much that He sent His Son to die for you.
And His Son, Jesus, loves YOU so much that He chose to die for you!
How does that make you feel?

For we wrestle not against flesh and blood,
but against principalities, against powers, against the rulers
of darkness of this world, against spiritual wickedness in
high places.

Ephesians 6:12 (KJV)

Be not overcome of evil, but overcome evil with good.

Romans 12:21 (KJV)

ACKNOWLEDGMENTS

A sincere thank you to the following:
My Lord and Savior, Jesus Christ.
My family – Thank you for all your support and
encouragement.
It means the world to me!

Special thanks to:
TreasureLine Publishing
My editors and beta readers
and last, but certainly NOT least
My Readers!
May your faith and trust in the Lord grow more every day!

ABOUT THE AUTHOR

Kelly Hagen is a wife and mother of three. She's also the author of the mystery romance series *Out Of the Past*:
Book One – Trent: Everyone Has A Past
Book Two – Haunted by the Past

You can find her on Facebook as well as Twitter
https://www.facebook.com/groups/207744259864995/
https://twitter.com/Kelly_Hagen

She'd love for you to check out her website, and while you're there send her message!
She'd love to hear from you!
https://kellyhagen.wixsite.com/author